THE NEW UNIT
COMMANDER—
Darryl Stevens' Story

Other books by Sue Cullins Walls
The Cat Who Couldn't Purr
Who Killed Norma Jean?
The Search
The Mystery of the Cabin in the Woods
The Unit Commander Book 2 Parts A and B

You my reach the author at suewalls1475@aol.com

THE NEW UNIT
COMMANDER—

Darryl Stevens' Story

FSC Series Book 3

Sue Cullins Walls

THE NEW UNIT COMMANDER—DARRYL STEVENS' STORY
FSC SERIES BOOK 3

iUniverse books may be ordered through booksellers or by contacting:

iUniverse
1663 Liberty Drive
Bloomington, IN 47403
www.iuniverse.com
1-800-Authors (1-800-288-4677)

ISBN: 978-1-5320-6184-4 (sc)
ISBN: 978-1-5320-6185-1 (e)

Print information available on the last page.

iUniverse rev. date: 12/11/2018

DEDICATION

TO MY SISTER, Joyce Price, for all of her encouragement and persistence. If not for her, this book would not have become a reality.

ACKNOWLEDGEMENTS

I WISH TO thank my husband, Harrison, again, for being so patient with me while I write my books. I also want to thank my sister, Joyce Price, again for her encouragement; my brother, John Cullins, for proofreading my books; my sister, Martha Cullins, for listening to my tales of woe and all of my family and friends for buying my books.

CHAPTER 1

DARRYL STEVENS HAD been with the Florida Federal Security Commission (FSC) for 10 years. He had started as soon as he graduated from high school at the age of 18. He had gone from the entry position of agent to the position of Second-in-Command (SIC) and now he was ready to be promoted to Unit Commander (UC). The only trouble was, there was no Unit Commander position available in Florida and probably wouldn't be for a long time. Since he didn't relish the idea of waiting for a position to open up in Florida, the only alternative was to move to a state where a position was already open.

Through his search for a Commander position, he found an open position in Arkansas. The position had been held for many years by Jim Ryan. He had heard of Jim Ryan; who hadn't? Jim Ryan was a legend throughout the whole country. Before his tragic death, his unit had been considered the best unit in the whole country.

Darryl saw that a man named Ted Ames had inherited the position, but was now retiring. Darryl knew that Mark Fuller had been Jim Ryan's SIC and had been given the position of Commander upon Jim's death. He also knew that, due to a tragic accident, Mark's position had been taken away from him and given to Ted Ames. Then, after Mark had recuperated, he was given the Commander position of another unit. Now that Mark's original unit was available,

Darryl wondered why he hadn't requested it. He figured that Mark must have gotten close to his new unit and now wanted to remain their Commander.

When Darryl had interviewed for the position of Unit Commander of that Unit, he was immediately hired in that position. Now, he was nervously preparing to move to Arkansas and start that job.

Darryl remembered meeting Mark Fuller when his unit came to Florida to assist Darryl's unit, led by Commander Greg Hendricks, a couple of times. Mark seemed like a nice guy, so Darryl hoped that he and Mark would become friends.

Darryl had heard that Jason Hall, Ted Ames' SIC, had also applied for the position of Commander of this Unit, but when he was offered the position of Commander in another Unit, he had taken it instead. Darryl had no idea why, but he was glad that he wouldn't be taking a unit away from someone else who had already been a member of that unit. He certainly didn't want to start a new job in a new state and have to cope with hard feelings from some of the team members. It would be hard enough starting a new job in a new state where everyone was a stranger to him.

Darryl had been to the office and introduced himself to the team. They seemed nice enough to him, but he still felt a chill in the room. Maybe there was someone else on the team who had aspirations of becoming the new Unit Commander. He hoped he was just imagining things, but still it was possible that he was stepping on someone else's toes.

He had arrived on Monday and contacted a Realtor on Tuesday. He had obtained a room in the barracks until he had found a place to live. He spent the week checking out houses and apartments. He finally settled on a large two-story wood-frame house that had been painted white by the previous owner. It was a little farther out of town than he had really wanted, but when he looked at it as it nestled quietly under the oaks and sweet gum trees, it seemed to call to him and say, "Welcome, come live with me and I will give you rest at the end of a long and trying day."

Darryl was glad that he had found the house before he started his new job. He didn't start for another week, so that would give him time to get moved in and buy some furniture and get settled before the trying task of getting started in a new job. He had to admit that he was nervous.

Mark Fuller must have sensed his unease, because he looked him up in the barracks and invited him to lunch. "We usually go to the McDonald's down the street for lunch," Mark said. "We can get in and out without using too much time. Sometimes we just barely have time to grab a sandwich before starting a new assignment."

"Thanks for inviting me, Mark," Darryl said. "I kinda feel at loose ends right now. I didn't realize how lonely I was going to be, so far away from my family and friends."

"You'll make new friends, soon, Darryl," Mark answered. "I'd like to invite you to come by my house and meet my family. My wife, Cat, would be happy to have you."

"Hey, Mark, whose your friend?" Cassidy Love asked, as she glided up to Mark's table. Cassidy had a sexy walk and when she walked, it seemed like she glided without touching the ground.

"Oh, Cassidy, I'd like for you to meet Darryl Stevens. He's the new Commander of Ted Ames' Unit. Darryl, this is my SIC, Cassidy Love."

"Well, Hel-lo, Cassidy," Darryl said slowly with a Southern drawl, dragging out hello. "Do you?"

"Do I what?" Cassidy asked, as she took Darryl's outstretched hand and gave him a sexy smile.

"Do you love?" Darryl asked, as he winked and gave her a sexy smile right back.

"Would you like to try me?" Cassidy asked, as she gave him a 'come on' look.

"I always like a good challenge," Darryl answered, still holding her hand.

3

"Will you two stop it?" Mark asked. "I don't have time for this. Cassidy, I'll see you later in my office. Now, Darryl, if you're having lunch with me, we need to get our food and eat so I can get back to work."

"I'm sorry, Mark," Darryl said a little embarrassed. "She seemed to be issuing a challenge and I couldn't let it pass. Is she married?"

"She's divorced, but you don't want to get involved with her. She's bad news," Mark answered.

"Maybe so," Darryl said. "I would still like to take her on."

"Suit yourself, Darryl," Mark said. "Don't say I didn't warn you when she chews you up and spits you out; she's a barracuda."

"She doesn't look all that dangerous to me," Darryl said, as he watched Cassidy sashay across the room.

"Just heed my warning and stay clear of her," Mark answered, as he carried his food to the table and sat down.

Darryl was still thinking about Cassidy as he sat down at the table opposite Mark. "Is she seeing anyone now?" he asked.

"Yes, I think she's seeing anyone who'll go out with her. You can't be seriously thinking about asking her out are you? Like I said, she's bad news," Mark said shaking his head.

"She looks like she'd be a lot of fun. Like I said, I like a good challenge and she looks like a good challenge," Darryl said, as he continued to watch Cassidy.

"Just don't say I didn't warn you," Mark insisted, and he changed the subject. "I don't know if you know it or not, but I was UC of that Unit before I had a bad accident."

"Yes, I'm aware of that, Mark," Darryl said. "I was wondering why you didn't go back to it, now that it's available."

"For one thing, I like where I am now, and for another thing, I thought that Jason Hall was going to take it," Mark answered, dipping a French fry in catsup and twisting it around lazily.

"Why didn't he take it?" Darryl asked, as he dipped a French fry into his catsup.

"I don't really know," Mark said. "I haven't really had a chance to talk to him yet. I'm sure he had a good reason because I know that he had wanted it." Then Mark finally quit swirling the fry in the catsup and popped it into his mouth.

Cassidy slid seductively up to the table and interrupted their conversation. "Well, I guess I better get back to the office; I'm afraid to be late. I have a hard nose for a UC, you know. Will I see you again, Darryl?"

"Yes, I hope so," Darryl said. "As a matter of fact, I was going to have a 'get acquainted' party for myself Friday night; can you come?"

"Sure, just tell me when and where and I'll be there," Cassidy said excitedly. "I never turn down an invitation to a good party."

"I have to be going, too," Mark said, as he rose and gave Cassidy a frown. "Don't be late, Cassidy. I need to see you in my office when you get back." Then he threw his trash into the trash container and walked angrily out the door.

"I think I made him mad," Darryl said, as he watched Mark's retreating figure.

"That's OK," Cassidy said. "I always make him mad. He and I are like vinegar and oil; we don't mix very well. Now, where and when is this party?"

Darryl gave Cassidy the directions to his new house and told her to be there about 7:00 p.m. "Why don't you bring some of your friends?" he asked. "I don't know anyone here and I sure would like to get acquainted with some people our age so I won't be so lonesome."

"I'll sure do that; I don't want you to get too friendly with them, though. I think I'd like to have you all to myself for a while," Cassidy said, as she put the piece of paper with Darryl's address on it into her cleavage.

"That sounds like a plan," Darryl said, as he stood and carried his trash to the trash bin. "I guess I need to go now, too. I have to get some furniture before Friday; I might need something for people to sit on."

"Don't worry too much about furniture," Cassidy said. "We can always sit on the floor."

"I guess I'll see you Friday night, then, bye until then," Darryl said, as he headed to his car, and turned and waved.

"Bye, I'll see you Friday night," Cassidy said, as she watched Darryl drive off. Then she hurried back to the office. She dreaded facing Mark, but she knew he couldn't chew her out for dating Darryl. Darryl wasn't a member of Mark's team, so he couldn't say anything to her about it.

At Cassidy's knock, Mark told her to come in and shut the door. "Before you start in on me, Mark, he isn't one of your team members. He belongs to another unit," Cassidy started before Mark could say anything.

"I know he isn't one of my team members, but I don't think he can handle someone like you," Mark answered, giving Cassidy a disapproving scowl.

"What do you mean by 'someone like me'?" she asked, the hurt showing in her voice.

"You know what I mean, Cassidy," Mark started. "He's younger than you are. He probably has never experienced anyone like you. You know what I mean. Leave him alone; he's a stranger here. He's probably lonely and he thinks you'll help him get over his loneliness. I know you, though. You'll just use him and toss him away with a broken heart. Leave him alone."

"He doesn't seem all that inexperienced to me, Mark," Cassidy said. "I think he can hold his own with me. Besides, he started it. As the saying goes, I don't think this is his first rodeo. I know a player when I see him and he is definitely a player."

"Well, he doesn't seem like a player, as you call it, to me. He seems like a little boy who is away from home for the first time and is lonely and just wants to find some friends. Like I said before, leave him alone."

"You can't order me to stay away from him, Mark," Cassidy said, getting angry. "I do as you say and I don't date any of the guys on our team, even though there is one I would like to date. But you can't tell me who I can and can't date outside of our team. Now, I'm going to that party Friday night and you can't stop me; so don't even try." Then she stalked out the door and slammed it behind her.

"Cassidy Love, I still think I made a mistake in keeping you on my team, no matter how good you are," Mark said to himself, as he slammed a file folder onto his desk and tried to concentrate on the assignment at hand.

CHAPTER 2

BY FRIDAY NIGHT, Darryl had purchased a sofa and chairs for the den; a kitchen table and chairs for the kitchen; a long dining room table and eight chairs for the dining room; and beds and dressers for the three bedrooms upstairs. There was a room downstairs that had probably originally been a bedroom, but he intended to make it his office later. Right now, all he had in it was a brown leather sofa, in case he had more guests spending the night than he anticipated. He would purchase a desk and computer later. He had drinks and snacks stored in the pantry off the kitchen. He had no idea how many people were coming, but he bought plenty and hoped it would be sufficient. He had posted an invitation on the bulletin board in the barracks and another one in the break room in the FSC Building. He had set up a stereo system and had a variety of music available. There was room for dancing in the middle of the large den, because he had arranged the seats around the wall and left the middle vacant in case the people wanted to dance.

At 6:00, Darryl looked around at all of his arrangements and felt satisfied that he had done everything that he needed for a successful "get acquainted" party.

There was a knock on the door and Darryl went to answer it, anxiously expecting his first guest. He looked through the small side window and, to his pleasant surprise, saw Cassidy Love and two other girls standing outside on the porch.

"Hi, come on in," Darryl said, as he opened the door wide and gave them a welcome smile. "Am I glad to see you," he said, as he gave Cassidy a quick kiss on the cheek.

"That's not how we welcome guests in Arkansas," Cassidy said and she grabbed him and gave him a kiss that curled his toes.

"Wow," Darryl said. "I like the way you welcome someone here. Come on in and find a seat. I have drinks in the fridge and snacks on the counter in the kitchen; help yourself."

"Darryl, this is Candy, Rita and Rose. Girls, this is Darryl Stevens. He's our new Unit Commander. He's just moved here from Florida and he doesn't know anyone. Make him feel welcome," Cassidy said.

"We certainly will," the girls all said in unison, as they all tried to hug him at the same time.

Candy was a slim blonde, who probably stood 5'7" in her bare feet. She walked sexily over to the sofa and sat down. "Come on girls, this is nice," she said.

Rita and Rose, both dark-haired, short, maybe 5'3" tall, with equally slim figures, moved gracefully over to the sofa and sat down beside Candy.

As the time got closer to 7:00, more guests arrived and the party became louder. Someone found the music and turned it on too loudly. Darryl turned it down some, but each time he turned it down, someone would turn it back up again. He was beginning to feel that things were getting out of hand, when there was a loud knock at the door. When he opened the door, there stood two uniformed policemen.

"Are you in charge here?" one of the policemen asked in a gruff voice.

"Yes, I am," Darryl answered, getting nervous.

"Will you please come outside so we can talk to you?" the

policeman asked, as he turned and walked back out onto the porch and expected Darryl to follow him.

"Sure," Darryl said, as he stepped out onto the porch and shut the door behind him.

"I'm sorry, Sir, but you're going to have to tone it down a bit," the policeman said.

"I'm sorry, Sir, but I'm trying. I've tried, but no one will listen to me," Darryl tried to shout over the loud noise.

"Well, if you can't do something, I'm going to have to do something myself," the police officer said. "I know you're way out in the country, but you're still disturbing someone else. There's been a complaint, so you have to tone it down. Do you understand?"

"Yes, Sir, I understand. Who complained? There's no one else here except that house over there and I didn't know anyone lived there," Darryl said, pointing to the house next door.

"Well, someone does live there and she doesn't like all the noise," the police officer answered. "Now, can you do something about it or do I have to?"

Just as Darryl was about to answer the policeman, Mark Fuller walked up on the porch behind the officers.

"Is something wrong Officer Hadley?" Mark asked one of the policemen.

"Oh, hello, Mark," the officer answered. "Yes, there's been a complaint about the noise here. I was just informing this gentleman that if he couldn't control his party, then I would be forced to do it myself."

"Why don't you let me give it a try?" Mark asked. "Do you mind if I try, Darryl?"

"No, I wish you would," Darryl answered quickly before the policemen acted.

Mark strode into the den, found the source of the music and turned it off. Everyone immediately stopped talking when the music stopped. "Listen up, everyone," Mark began. "Darryl invited you to his home to welcome him to our fair state. I think each of you should be ashamed of yourselves. Instead of welcoming him, you've ruined his beautiful home and disturbed his neighbors to the extent that they probably won't like having him live here. Therefore, he will be unwelcome in his neighborhood. Now, it's getting late and it's a long drive back to town. Why don't each of you apologize to Darryl and take your leave? You can also tell him welcome and thank him for the nice party as you go by. If you see some trash on the floor, you can also pick it up and put it into the trash can as you go by. That way you can help him clean up. Now, let's get going. Tell Darryl thanks and goodbye."

Everyone ducked their heads; picked up a piece of trash; thanked Darryl for the party; said welcome and headed for the door.

Soon, Mark, Cassidy and her three friends were the only ones left in the house. The policemen thanked Mark, warned Darryl not to have anymore loud parties and left.

"Thanks, Mark," Darryl said. "I don't know how it got out of hand so fast. I thought I was in control, but I wasn't."

"That's OK, Darryl," Mark said. "You just don't know this bunch, yet. I thought you might have trouble, that's why I came by. Once you get your feet planted, you'll be able to handle it better. Cassidy, I think you and your friends need to leave, too."

"Well, I think you need to mind your own business, Mark Fuller," Cassidy said sarcastically. "I'm not at the office now and I don't have to obey your orders."

Mark didn't say anything, but he gave Cassidy a glare that said he would gladly strangle her if he could.

"That's OK, Cassidy," Darryl said. "Why don't you go now. We can get together some other time, just the two of us, OK?"

"Sure, Darryl, we'll go, but not because Mark said for us to go. I'll see you around. Thanks for the party. I'm sorry that it got out of hand and the police had to break it up."

"Goodbye, Cassidy. It was nice to meet you Candy, Rose and Rita," Darryl said, as they walked out the door. "I'll see you all later."

"Thanks, Mark, I appreciate what you did," Darryl said. "I don't know what I would have done if you hadn't shown up. I sure didn't want the police to take care of it."

"That's OK, Darryl," Mark said, as he picked up a large garbage bag. "Now, let's get rid of some of this trash."

"You don't have to help clean up, Mark," Darryl said. "I can take care of that at least."

"It'll go faster if we do it together," Mark said, as he continued to pick up trash and put it into the bag. Soon, all of the trash had been picked up and every room had been straightened.

"I guess I'll go on home now, Darryl," Mark said, as he headed toward the door. "Welcome to our state and our FSC office. Sorry you had a bad experience at the beginning. Hopefully, this will be the worse experience you will have here. I'll see you Monday."

Mark started walking out the door, then he turned and said, "One more thing, Darryl. Be Careful of Cassidy Love. I was serious when I told you she would chew you up and spit you out. She really will. Good night. See you later."

Darryl watched Mark walk to his car. "That's some man," he thought. "I don't know what I would have done if he hadn't shown up. I sure hope I never have to compete with him for anything. I know I'd lose. I wonder if Cassidy Love ever chewed him up and spit him out. I kinda doubt it. I guess I might better take to heart what he said, though. I don't think I could stand up to her like he does. This job may turn out to be more than I expected. I haven't even started yet and I already have doubts. I guess I'll see."

He looked toward the house next door and saw a light in an upstairs bedroom window. It looked like someone standing there looking out at him as he walked back into the house. He had never seen anyone there before. He thought it was a vacant house. He would have to walk over tomorrow and apologize for the noise. He didn't want to start out on the wrong foot with his only neighbor. Then he walked slowly up the stairs and started getting ready for bed. He was so tired. He sure hoped things got better from now on.

CHAPTER 3

THE NEXT MORNING, Darryl was up early, even though he had slept only four hours.

He staggered down to the kitchen and made a pot of coffee. He was already developing a headache and hoped that the coffee would stop it before it became a full-blown head-pounding throb.

He heated up a couple of slices of pizza that were left over from the night before. He ate the pizza and washed it down with the coffee and called it breakfast. He felt bad about disturbing his only neighbor last night and he wanted to go over early and issue an apology to them.

He made his way through the maze of hedge that separated his yard from the neatly manicured lawn next door and stopped in front of the house. There were five steps leading up to a generous porch that looked as though it wrapped around the entire house. The house was an enormous, old, wooden house, built in the old Southern plantation style. It was painted white with black trim. "I've always wanted a porch like that," Darryl thought, as he made his way up to the front door. He rang the bell and looked around while he waited for someone to answer the door.

Over to his left was a large swing that was suspended from the ceiling by two heavy chains. The swing looked as if it was large enough to hold three or four people at one time. He had a desire to sit in it and test it out, but just as he turned toward the swing, he heard someone reaching the door and saw it slowly open.

There she was in all of her glory---A full six feet two inches and approximately two hundred pounds of her! He gulped as he took in the sight of her. From the top of her silver-gray hair, that was cut in a becoming style, all the way down to her stylish blouse and slacks and matching sandals. She reminded him of an elementary school teacher he once had. He could almost hear Miss Deimer say, "Darryl Stevens, if you don't sit down and behave, I'm sending you to the principal's office." The woman was leaning on a wooden cane, but Darryl could almost imagine her standing there with a frown on her face, holding a ruler in her hand, getting ready to smack him with it.

"May I help you?" the woman asked in a voice that was softer than he had imagined it to be.

"Yes, I'm...I'm...My name is Darryl Stevens, your new neighbor," he finally managed to stammer out. "I want to apologize to you for last night."

"Come in, Darryl," she said, as she turned and walked back down the hall. She expected Darryl to follow her, so he cautiously walked through the door and shut it behind him.

"Come in and have a seat," the woman said, indicating a comfortable-looking chair in what Darryl figured was the den. There was a comfortable-looking sofa and several nice recliners placed attractively around the room. There was a nice brick fireplace at one end of the room and the chairs all faced it. There were several end tables placed strategically at the end of the sofa and between the chairs and each one held a beautiful Tiffany lamp. He glanced quickly around the room and saw several pieces of art. (He didn't know anything about art, but he figured they were probably valuable.)

"My name is Joyce Fowler, but everyone calls me Miss Joy. You may call me that, if you wish," she said, bringing Darryl out of his assessment of the room. "Now, what was that you wanted to tell me?"

"I just wanted to apologize to you for disturbing you last night. I just moved here from Florida and will be starting a new job Monday. I just invited the people I'll be working with. I don't really know them, so I didn't know how wild they were. I'll be more selective next time. Again, I'm sorry that the noise disturbed you."

"I accept your apology, Darryl," Miss Joy said. "I always like to get along with my neighbors, but your party was a might too wild. I couldn't even hear my TV. I finally gave it up and went to bed, but I couldn't go to sleep. I'm sorry I had to call the law on you, but I just couldn't take it any longer."

"That's OK, Miss Joy. I tried to get them to quiet down, but they just ignored me. Finally between the police and Mark Fuller, they finally did."

"Oh, was Mark over there?" Miss Joy asked with a surprised voice.

"He came when the police did," Darryl said. "He wasn't there when the party was so wild, though. I don't want you to get the wrong idea about Mark. He was the one who got my party under control."

"I didn't think Mark would be at a wild party like that," Miss Joy said. "He and his family go to church with me. I didn't think he was that kind of person."

"No, Miss Joy, Mark isn't, as you put it, 'that kind of person.' I don't want you to get the wrong idea about Mark," Darryl hurriedly said.

"Well, I know Mark and I didn't think he would be there. Speaking of church," she said abruptly changing the subject. "Have you found a church yet? If not, I would like to invite you to go to church with me in the morning. I go to a little Baptist Church down the road. Everyone is very friendly and I know they would be glad to have you."

"Thank you for the invitation, Miss Joy, but I'm sorry, I can't. I'll be very busy tomorrow. I start my new job Monday and I have a lot I need to do before Monday. As a matter of fact, I need to go and get started on it now. Thanks for the invitation, though," Darryl said, as he rose to go.

Miss Joy followed him to the door and again invited him to go to church with her the next day. "I usually go to Sunday School and church, but if you want to go with me, we can just go to church so you can get acquainted with everyone," she said, as he walked out the door.

"Thanks, again, Miss Joy, but I don't think I'll have time," Darryl said over his shoulder, as he hurried toward the hedge. He gave a sigh, as he came out of the maze on his side of the hedge. "Boy, that lady is persistent," he said to himself, as he climbed the stairs to his own house.

He gave a satisfied smile to his front door. His father had made a career of the military and Darryl had spent most of his life traveling from place to place. He was hoping this house would be his home for a long time to come. He had just finished making peace with his neighbor, so he hoped he wouldn't have any neighbor troubles. "Yes," he thought. "I think I'm gonna like it here."

The next morning, Darryl was planning to sleep late, but he was awakened by the insistent grinding of a car starter. He listened for a few minutes and then he realized it was Miss Joy's car and it probably wasn't going to start.

He jumped out of bed and slipped his feet into the slippers he had sitting next to the bed and pulled on a pair of pants. He didn't even bother to grab a shirt. He ran through the maze of hedges and over to the car. "Hold on, Miss Joy," he said, as he tapped on the driver's side window. "Stop, let me look under the hood."

"Oh, Darryl," she said. "Thank you, I didn't know what to do. It won't start."

"Pull the hood latch," Darryl said, as he went around to the front of the car and prepared to open the car's hood. After opening the hood, he inspected the battery cables and found that they were pretty corroded. He took his pocket knife and scraped off what he could get off and then replaced the cables. "Now, Miss Joy, try to start it again," he said.

This time, it started.

"Thank you, Darryl," she said, as she looked approvingly at his bare muscular chest and arms. "Now that you're up, why don't you go to church with me?" she asked.

"I really have a lot to do today, Miss Joy, but thanks again for the invitation. You probably need to get some new battery cables. That may be your problem."

He started toward the hedge and heard Miss Joy start backing out of the driveway. At the end of the driveway, the car died. He turned to watch, as she tried to start it again. He heard her crank it several times, but the car still refused to start. He walked slowly to the end of the driveway and told her to open the hood again. He repeated the process of scraping the battery cables and the battery posts.

"Try starting it again, Miss Joy," he said. "Your battery may be going bad, Miss Joy," Darryl said. "I think you should take your car to your mechanic and let him check it out. Do you have a regular mechanic?"

"Yes, I do, Darryl, but can't you fix it for me? You seem to know what you're doing," she answered hopefully.

"I'm not a mechanic," Darryl answered. "I just know the basic things to do when a car won't start. You still need to take it to your mechanic."

"Well, I guess I better be going and let you get back to your important business," Miss Joy said a little sarcastically. "I don't know what I'll do if it won't start after church."

Her sarcasm wasn't lost on Darryl. "OK, Miss Joy," he said, after a loud sigh. "If you'll wait long enough for me to get dressed, I'll go to church with you."

She happily said of course she would wait.

As Darryl made his way back through the hedge maze, he said

to himself, "She must have done something to that car to get me to go with her and I fell for it."

He hurried up stairs, pulled a shirt out of his closet and buttoned it, as he raced down the stairs. He jumped into the passenger's seat and Miss Joy took off down the road fast enough to spray gravel behind her.

"I'm glad you're going with me," Miss Joy said. "Now I won't be afraid that I'll be stranded somewhere. I think you'll like our church, too. Everyone is so friendly. Mark Fuller and his family go there, so it won't be like you won't know anyone."

At the church, Miss Joy introduced Darryl to Rev. Baxter and several others, then she spotted Mark Fuller. "Mark, I think you know my guest," she said, as she walked over to where Mark was sitting with his family.

"Hello, Darryl," Mark said, as he turned around and saw Darryl standing next to Miss Joy.

"Cat, Honey, I would like you to meet our new Unit Commander, Darryl Stevens. Darryl, this is my wife, Cat, our son Jimmy Ryan and our daughter, Crystal."

"Hello, Darryl," Cat said, as she extended her hand in a warm greeting. "It's a pleasure to meet you. Welcome."

"Thank you, Mrs. Fuller," Darryl answered. "Jimmy Ryan? Your son's name is Jimmy Ryan?"

"Yes," Mark answered. "Before you ask, yes, he's named after Jim Ryan. Cat was Jim's widow. We wanted to honor his memory by naming our first son after him.

"I would also like to introduce you to my sister-in-law, Carol Taylor; her husband, Skip; daughter Sherry Rene and their son, Trey."

Skip and Carol said, "Hello and welcome to our church." Then Sherry Rene said, "Hello, Mr. Darryl, I'm pleased to meet you."

As Miss Joy and Darryl sat down in the pew behind him, Mark turned around and whispered, "Sherry Rene is a very precocious child. She's eight going on 20, if you know what I mean. Be careful, she can see right into your very soul."

Then everyone stopped talking because it was time for services to start.

After church was over, Mark asked if Miss Joy and Darryl would like to join them for lunch.

"That would be fine with me, if it's OK with Darryl," Miss Joy said.

Even though Darryl would have liked to have gone on home, he said it was OK with him, too.

As they were eating, Jason Hall came over to speak to them. "Hello, Mark, everyone," he said.

"Hello, Jason, I'm glad you're here," Mark said. "I'd like for you to meet our new Unit Commander, Darryl Stevens. Darryl, this is Jason Hall. Jason was the SIC under Ted Ames."

"It's nice to meet you, Jason," Darryl said, as he extended his hand to Jason. "I heard that you were first choice for my job. May I ask what happened?"

"I don't want to discuss it right now," Jason said. "I'll tell you about it some other time when we're alone."

With that, Jason said, "I'll see you later." Then he went back to his table.

About 3:00 Monday morning, Darryl was shaken out of bed by a loud clap of thunder that sounded as if it was right above his bedroom. He awoke to a brilliant display of lightning followed by rapid claps of thunder. Then the rain started. The rain came down in buckets. Darryl had never seen it rain so hard and so fast. "Just what I need on the day I begin a new job," Darryl moaned. "I hope it quits before I have to leave for work." Then he gave a disgusted sigh, pulled his pillow over his head and tried to go back to sleep.

That was almost impossible, though. With his head under the pillow and his eyes closed, he couldn't see the lightning, but he could still hear the crashing of the thunder and the rain pelting the window.

Finally, at 6:00, he dragged himself out of bed and downstairs to the kitchen. The thunder and lightening had finally decreased to a low rumble, but the rain continued to come down in sheets. "This looks like the hurricane I sometimes encountered while living in Florida," he thought.

He turned on the TV to get the weather. The forecast was for a chance of rain every day that week. It also looked like a 100% chance of rain for that day. "Just what I need today of all days," Darryl mumbled to himself, as he measured coffee and water into the coffee maker.

When the coffee was ready, Darryl poured a cup and sipped on it while he scrambled a couple of eggs, fried two slices of bacon and made some toast. "I guess I had better eat a good breakfast," he thought. "I'll need something to help me combat that rain."

By 7:00 a.m., he was ready to leave, but dreaded going out into the rain. He was thankful that it had slacked up slightly. "Maybe it'll stop in a few minutes," he hoped. Sure enough, by the time he stepped out the door, it had slowed to a drizzle.

When Darryl reached his office, there was no one else there yet, so he looked up Mark Fuller's office. He found Mark already in his office doing some paperwork. "Good morning, Mark," Darryl said, as he knocked on his office door.

"Hello, Darryl," Mark said, as he looked up to see who it was. "Come on in and sit down. How is everything going?"

"I don't know yet," Darryl answered. "I just got here and no one is in the office, yet. I just thought I'd come by and say hello to a friendly face before I get started."

"Well, I'm sure everyone will be friendly to you," Mark said. "I worked with most of that bunch and I never had any problems with them. I would have taken it over again, but I'm too involved with this unit now. Also, I thought Jason was going to take it. I'm surprised that he didn't. I'll have to ask him about that the next time I see him."

"Well, I'm glad he didn't take it or I might not have been able to get a Commander's position," Darryl answered.

As Mark's unit members started to slowly arrive, Darryl said, "I guess I better be getting back to my office. Maybe some of my members will be arriving soon."

Just then Cassidy Love arrived. She saw Darryl standing in the doorway of Mark's office and stopped to say hello. "Hello, you good-looking hunk," she said, as she patted him on the back.

"Good morning, Cassidy, thanks for the compliment," Darryl answered.

"Are you slumming?" she asked.

"I just needed to see a friendly face before I face my unit," Darryl answered. "I'm glad I caught you. Would you like to have dinner with me Friday night?"

"Yes, I would love to go to dinner with you Friday night," she answered, as she looped her arm into his arm and gave him a sexy smile.

"Give me your address and I'll pick you up about 6:00 p.m. Will that be OK?" Darryl asked.

"Sure, here's my address and my telephone number, just in case something happens and you can't make it," she answered, as she handed him a piece of paper.

"I better be going now," he said, as he walked out the door. Then he leaned over and gave her a quick kiss on the lips. "See you later, Doll."

When Darryl was gone, Mark asked Cassidy to step into his office.

"All right, Mark, before you start," she said before Mark could say anything. "I'm not going to hurt him. I think he's a big boy and I can tell he's been around a few women like me. I don't think you need to worry about him."

"OK, Cassidy," Mark said. "I just wanted to caution you. Remember that both of you will still be working in this same building come Monday morning. Don't do something that will embarrass either of you. Remember that he's just starting a new job and will need to pay full attention to it. I just wanted to offer you a little advice. If you don't want to take it, that's your choice. I just thought I'd try to stop something that might get out of hand."

"Well, thanks for the advice, Mark," she said sarcastically. "Just don't feel hurt if I don't take it. In the future, stay out of my business. Sometimes I feel like you think you own me, just because I work under you. I want to make it clear to you that you don't. I also want to make it clear to you that you're not my big brother or my father, so stay out of my love life, OK?"

With that, she tilted her head up and marched out of the door of Mark's office and straight to her own desk.

CHAPTER 4

WHEN DARRYL ARRIVED back at his own office, his team members had begun to straggle into the office one by one. He greeted them as they walked through the door. Some of them mumbled a weak hello, but most of them just ignored him. Most of them had attended his party on Saturday night and were embarrassed at the way it had ended.

When everyone had arrived, Darryl called a meeting in the conference room. "I think I've met every one of you, but just in case there's someone I missed, my name is Darryl Stevens. I worked for 10 years with the Florida FSC. I think I worked with some of you a couple of times when my Commander requested your help on a difficult assignment. I was SIC to my Commander for the past six years. During that time, I served as Commander due to my UC's illness. In case you were thinking I'm a novice with no experience as UC, I can show you my record, if you require it.

"I may not do things as you have been used to doing them. If you see that you have a better way to do them, let me know. We can compare the two methods and choose the one that best serves our purpose. I'm not hard to get along with. I do demand your respect and obedience, though. After all, I am your Commander. I don't want you to ever forget that. Don't let the fact that I'm from Florida cloud your judgment. Whether you like me or not it doesn't really matter. I'm still your Commander and I do deserve your respect. Now, are there any questions?"

"Yes, Sir," Ben Johnson said.

"Your name is?" Darryl asked.

"Ben Johnson, Sir," he answered.

"What is your question?" Darryl asked.

"What happened to Jason Hall?" Ben asked. "I thought he was going to be our UC. Did you pull some strings and kick him out?"

"I have no idea what happened to Jason Hall," Darryl said getting angry. "I'm sorry, but I don't even know Jason Hall. I only met him briefly Sunday at a restaurant. If you want to know something about him, you need to ask him, not me. Now, are there any questions that I can answer? If not, then you're dismissed to go to your desks and complete your tasks."

Everyone stood and filed out in front of Darryl. Some of them grumbled quietly, as they passed Darryl, who gave each of them a stern look. "I hope this doesn't turn out to be a mistake," Darryl thought, as he looked at the disgruntled group. "It looks like it's going to be more difficult than I had imagined. Oh, well, I'm here now, I'll have to bear the consequences. I just hope it gets better." Then he went into his office and started going over the case files. He wanted to familiarize himself with the assignments that his unit had done in the past. That way, he would know what to expect in the future.

In reading the most recent case files, Darryl noticed that most of his unit's assignments had been local or at least in the United States. He also noted that, when Jim Ryan and Mark Fuller had been Commander, most of their assignments had been outside the United States. He wondered what had caused the change. He also noticed that everyone in his unit had obtained two weeks of training at the Training Academy in Jonesboro. He made a note to check into obtaining the same training. He saw where it was required for each of the Arkansas Units, but Florida had no special requirement. He wanted to get the training as soon as he could.

As he was reading the files, there was a knock on his door.

When he looked up, Ben Johnson was standing there. "Commander Stevens, may I come in?"

"Sure, Ben, come on in and shut the door," Darryl answered. "Have a seat. What can I do for you?"

"Sir, I want to apologize to you for my question. I guess I was sore because I thought you probably knew someone high up like Director Halbert, and got him to put you in ahead of Jason. I really like Jason and I thought he was getting a raw deal. If that isn't the case, then I apologize and I'll be happy to work under you."

"Thank you, Ben," Darryl answered. "I appreciate that. No, I don't know anyone high up who would help me get this job. I only met Director Halbert when I came for an interview. Like I said, I don't have any idea why he decided not to take this unit. I only know that he was their first choice and I was their second choice. I only got the job when Jason turned it down. Now, does that satisfy you?"

"Yes, thanks, Sir," Ben said, as he rose to go. "I appreciate your candid answer." Then Ben went back to his desk and Darryl finished reading the case files.

As Darryl pulled into his driveway that afternoon, he could see Miss Joy and a man in front of her house. It looked as if the man had a shovel and seemed to be digging a ditch. Miss Joy was standing over him and it looked as if she was chewing him out or either telling him how to do what he was doing.

When she saw Darryl, she called out to him. "Hello, Darryl, can you come over here for a few minutes?"

Darryl was exhausted. He had had a very trying day and all he wanted to do was go into his house, pull off his shoes, fix a glass of iced tea and lean back in his recliner and rest. He gave a loud sigh and went through the hedge and down to where Miss Joy was standing.

"Did you need something, Miss Joy?" he asked.

"See all the water that's still here from the rain this morning," she said, as she swept her arm across the front lawn. "I hired Mr. Harris, here, to dig a drainage ditch to get rid of it for me. I think it should go that direction," she said indicating a westerly direction. "And he seems to think it should go the other way. What do you think?"

"Has Mr. Harris ever done this before?" Darryl asked, looking toward Mr. Harris for an answer.

"Well, I suppose so," she answered and Mr. Harris nodded his head to indicate that yes, he had done it before.

"Then I think you should do as Mr. Harris said," Darryl answered. "Then if it doesn't work, make him come back and do it over again."

"That's a great idea," Miss Joy said with a smile. "OK, Mr. Harris, you do it your way and, as Darryl said, if it doesn't work, you can just come back and do it over free of charge."

Darryl headed toward the hedge, but at the entrance to the maze, he stopped and turned around. "Mr. Harris, would you do the same thing to my yard?" Darryl asked. "When you finish, come knock on my door and I'll pay you."

"Sure thing, Mr. Stevens, I'll be glad to do that," Mr. Harris said with a smile.

Then Darryl continued on toward his house and let out a big sigh. He was fond of Miss Joy, but she was becoming a pain. He hoped it wouldn't be that way the whole time he lived here.

Two days later when Darryl pulled into his driveway, he saw Miss Joy sitting on a riding lawn mower attempting to start it. She was having just as much trouble starting the lawn mower as she had starting her car on Sunday.

"Hold on, Miss Joy, stop!" he shouted, as he ran up to the lawn mower. "Miss Joy, what are you doing?" he asked.

"Can't you see?" Miss Joy shouted angrily. "I'm trying to start this blasted machine, but it isn't cooperating."

"If you'll pull the hood latch, I'll look and see if I can see what's wrong," he said, as he waited for her to obey.

Under the hood, he could see that the battery cables were just as corroded as the car cables had been. He took his pocket knife and scraped the cables like he had done for the car. "Now try again, Miss Joy," he said.

The engine sputtered a little, kicked off and immediately died again. "Miss Joy, if you'll give me time to go change clothes, I'll come back and try again."

"OK," she answered. "Don't take too long, though. I need to get my lawn cut so I can go prepare dinner."

"I'll be back in a few minutes," Darryl said, as he headed toward the hedge. "That woman will be the death of me yet," he muttered, as he hurried into his house and up the stairs to his bedroom. A few minutes later, he emerged, wearing shorts and a T-shirt.

"Now, Miss Joy, you go sit on the porch in your swing and I'll start the mower and mow the grass for you," he said, as he urged her off the mower and gave her a gentle push toward the porch.

"Darryl, you don't have to mow my grass for me," she said, as she turned and headed back toward the mower. "I'm capable of mowing my own grass."

"I know you are, Miss Joy, but I'd like to mow it for you. Is that OK with you?" Then the mower kicked off and was purring like a kitten. "Now, Miss Joy, you do as I say and I'll mow the grass," he said, as he put the mower in gear and started cutting a swatch of grass.

"I'll go fix dinner, then," Miss Joy shouted, as she walked up the steps. At the top of the stairs, she turned and watched Darryl for a few minutes. "You are a gorgeous hunk of man," she muttered, as she approvingly watched as he easily mowed down one strip and up another one. "My niece needs to meet you," she said to herself. "You're just the man she needs."

About an hour later, Darryl pulled the mower into Miss Joy's garage and walked to her door and knocked. He had gotten hot and pulled off his T-shirt and his chest and back were covered in sweat.

Miss Joy figured Darryl was the one who was knocking, so she called out for him to come on inside. "I have dinner ready," she said, as she turned and saw him. "Oh, my," she said. "You are a nice figure of a man."

Darryl turned red from embarrassment, but he said, "Thank you, Miss Joy. Coming from you, I would consider that a compliment."

"It was meant to be a compliment," Miss Joy said. "Didn't you say that you had never been married?"

"Yes, Miss Joy," Darryl said, as he backed out the door. "I have never been nor do I ever want to be married, even though my mother would love to have grandchildren, she'll just have to settle for the ones my sister gave her. Now, if you'll excuse me, I need to go shower."

"Darryl, I have a wonderful niece, who would be just perfect for you," Miss Joy started.

"Miss Joy, before you start, I don't need anyone to play matchmaker for me. I'm a confirmed bachelor and I would appreciate it if you would stay out of my business."

"I didn't intend to make you mad, Darryl," Miss Joy hurriedly tried to smooth things over. "I just thought you might get lonesome in that big old house by yourself and I have a wonderful niece."

"Again let me emphasize, Miss Joy," Darryl said trying to hold his temper. "I am a confirmed bachelor. I do not intend to get married. I like my life the way it is, so just butt out, OK? Now, I have to go get a shower."

"I'm sorry, if I made you mad, Darryl," she said apologetically. "If you'll forgive me, I'd appreciate it. I have some chicken and dumplings cooked, if you would like to come back and have dinner with me."

"I would love to have dinner with you, if you promise to stay out of my business," Darryl said. "I love chicken and dumplings. If you want to wait until I shower, I'll be back shortly."

"I'll wait for you. You go on and get your shower," Miss Joy said. She watched as Darryl hurried out the door and through the hedge. "My, what a shame to waste such great husband material on a confirmed bachelor. Darryl may not realize it, but his bachelor days are coming to an end."

CHAPTER 5

DARRYL AWOKE FRIDAY morning nervous about his date with Cassidy Love. He had dated many women before, but none of them had come close to the attraction he had for Cassidy. He had already made a reservation for 7:30 p.m. at a fancy restaurant downtown. He had purchased a corsage, made with pink carnations, for her and it was waiting for her in his refrigerator at home. He had even taken his best black suit to the cleaners and now it was hanging in his bedroom awaiting the time for him to put it on.

He hurried down the stairs and drove to the office as quickly as he could. He thought that if he started early, maybe the day would go faster and soon it would be time to pick her up. He couldn't have been any more wrong if he had tried.

The day started off badly to begin with. Director Halbert called and told him to come to his office. He wanted to discuss the fact that Darryl hadn't had the two-week training that was now required for each unit member.

"When we hired you, Commander Stevens, it was my impression that you had already completed your two-week training at an academy in Florida, isn't that correct?" Director Halbert asked after Darryl had come into his office and sat down where the Director had indicated.

"Yes, Sir, I have completed training that was required in Florida, but I have discovered that your Academy is far more advanced than ours. I intend to attend the Academy in Jonesboro as soon as I can, but I wanted a few weeks to get settled and become familiar with the unit before I left for two weeks. I thought that would be best. Is that not correct, Sir?" Darryl answered.

"That's good, but I want you to have the training before you lead your unit out on an assignment," Director Halbert said. "You need to be able to follow the same procedure that your unit is following. I need to get your unit back out on the field as soon as possible, because it's one of the best that I have. At least it was when Jim Ryan was alive. Anyway, you need to get that training as soon as possible."

"Yes, Sir, I'll make the arrangements as soon as I can," Darryl said.

"You may go now," Director Halbert said. "Just be sure and get that training ASAP."

"Yes, Sir," Darryl said and he walked out the door. He let out a loud sigh, as he cleared the doorway. He hadn't realized it, but he had been holding his breath. "Well, that was a good start to my day," he thought, as he made his way back to his office. "What else is going to go wrong?"

His answer came sooner than he had expected. He had just gotten back to his office and sat down at his desk when Scott Harding knocked on his door.

"Come in, Scott and close the door," Darryl said in an exasperated voice. "What can I do for you?"

"I was just wondering if you had decided on who your SIC is going to be," Scott started.

"No, I haven't, Scott," Darryl answered. "I haven't had a chance to assess each member's abilities. Who was SIC for Commander Ames?"

"Jason Hall was Commander Ames' SIC. Then, when he retired, I thought Jason would be Commander, but it seems like I was wrong," Scott said sarcastically.

"I guess you were wrong," Darryl replied. "So, who do you think should be my SIC?"

"Well, I would really like that position," Scott answered.

"Do you have any experience as an SIC?" Darryl asked.

"Yes, I filled in for Jason a few times. I did it enough to know what to do if I was in charge," Scott answered.

"When I have time, I'll assess you as well as the other members of the unit and I'll give the position to the one I feel is most qualified. I can't make a decision until I've assessed everyone's abilities, though. I will tell you this, though, Director Halbert wants me to take the two-weeks training at the Academy as soon as possible. I may need you to fill in for me during that time, if you're willing."

"Sure, I'll be glad to do it," Scott said. "Like I said, I've filled in before."

"OK, if that's all you wanted, I need to get back to work," Darryl said.

"Sure, that's all I wanted. I'll go back to my desk, now," Scott said, as he opened the office door and left.

Finally, Darryl made it through several irritating incidents and it was time to go home. He hurried upstairs and into the shower. He carefully dressed in his best Sunday suit that had come fresh from the cleaners. When he was satisfied that he looked as good as he could possibly look, he hurried down the stairs and retrieved the corsage from the fridge. Now he was ready to go. He looked at his watch and saw that it was 6:30 p.m. He knew it would take him at least 30 minutes to drive to Cassidy's house, so without further delay, he hurried to his car and headed downtown.

He whistled as he drove. The song that he whistled was an old song, but it fit his mood. "Got a date with an angel. Got to meet her at seven. Got a date with an angel and I'm on my way to heaven."* He sang the words now and then. He had heard his father sing that song sometimes when he was getting dressed to take his mother to

---

* Got A Date With An Angel" Lyrics by Clifford Grey and Sammy Miller

dinner. It always stuck in his mind and this seemed like a good time for him to sing it.

He arrived at her apartment in good spirits and knocked on her door. When she opened the door, he caught his breath. She was even more beautiful than she had been the first day he had seen her. "Hello, Cassidy," he was finally able to stammer out.

"Hello, Darryl, come in," she said, stepping aside so he could enter.

"You look lovely," he said, as he handed her the corsage. "This is for you."

"Why, thank you, Darryl. I don't think I've ever had a date bring me a corsage," she said. "Will you help me put it on?"

"Sure," he said, as he tried to figure out a place to put his hands that would be safe. When he finally got the corsage pinned to her dress, he asked if she was ready to go.

"Sure, just let me grab my bag and I'll be ready," she answered, as she hurried into the bedroom to retrieve it.

As he took her arm and walked her to his car, he couldn't believe his luck. He never dreamed that he would find such a gorgeous woman so soon after arriving at his new home. He especially never dreamed that she would actually go on a date with him. "Yes," he thought. "I'll remember this date for a long time. I can hardly wait for the best part."

At the restaurant, he asked Cassidy if she would like some wine. When she said she would, he ordered a bottle. They took their time and enjoyed the food and the wine, even though Darryl was anxious to get Cassidy alone again.

It was 9:00 when they finally finished their meal. "Would you like to go to my place for a while?" Darryl asked. He was pretty sure her answer would be yes.

"I might as well," she answered, a little mellow because of the wine.

When they walked into Darryl's house, he indicated a seat in the den. "Sit down and I'll get us something to drink," he said, as he started toward the kitchen.

He came back with a glass of Coke for each of them and set them down on the coffee table. Then he sat down next to her on the sofa and put his arm around her shoulders. He leaned over and kissed her neck and ran his fingers seductively down her arm. When his hand reached her hand, he picked it up and lightly kissed the palm of her hand. When he felt Cassidy shiver at his touch, he kissed each of her finger tips.

His passion began to rise, as he kissed her neck and nibbled her ear. Then he whispered into her ear, "Would you like to see my bedroom?"

"You know, Darryl, you're about as subtle as being hit over the head with a sledge hammer," she said, as she pushed him away.

He was stunned. "You knew why I brought you here. I thought you wanted the same thing," he said, as his spirit began to plummet.

"Yes, I knew," she answered. "I just wanted to see how long it would take you to get me into bed."

"And was I too fast for you?" he asked sarcastically. "If you hadn't wanted it, then why did you advertise?"

"I wasn't advertising," she answered. "It was just as I suspected, although I thought you would at least court me first."

"I thought I had courted you a little," he said, as he leaned over and kissed her neck again. "Come to bed with me," he whispered in her ear, as he ran his fingers down her arm again. She shuddered and started to rise. He followed her and took her arm and led her to his bedroom.

In his bedroom, he leaned her gently across his bed and leaned down and kissed her lightly on her lips. He kissed her again a little more urgently. Then he leaned down and claimed her whole mouth in his. Kissing her was everything he had dreamed it would be. He certainly couldn't charge her with false advertisement. She was everything she led him to believe she was. He put his arm around her and drew her close to him and fell into a deep satisfied sleep.

He awoke when he felt her stir. He looked toward the window and saw that it was becoming daylight. He hadn't intended for her to stay all night. He jumped up and headed for the shower. After his shower, he wrapped a towel around his waist and walked over to the bed, as he dried his hair on another towel.

"Would you like to take a shower now?" he asked her, as she rolled over and smiled at him in a dreamy sort of way. "Yes, I would," she answered and rolled out of bed and headed for the shower.

When she was dressed, he said, "I would offer to fix breakfast for you, but I bet you're in a hurry to get home, aren't you?"

"I'm not in that big of a hurry," she answered. "Are you rushing me off?"

"Well, I really have a lot of things to do today," he said. He didn't want to confess to her that he didn't want his nosy neighbor to see him leaving with her. He hoped that he would be able to get her out of the house and into the car before Miss Joy was awake.

"You didn't seem like you were in such a hurry to get me home last night," Cassidy said. "What's your hurry this morning?"

"Like I said," he answered. "I have a lot to do today. I need to get you home, so I can get to it."

She was hurt, but she obediently followed him down the stairs and out the front door to the car.

"Good morning, Darryl. Are you just now getting home?" Miss Joy asked when she saw Darryl and Cassidy getting into Darryl's car.

"No, Miss Joy," Darryl answered. "I've been home all night." He knew that she had seen his car and knew that he had been at home.

"Is that your friend?" she asked, pointing to Cassidy.

"Yes, Miss Joy, this is Cassidy Love, a friend of mine. I'm just taking her home."

Miss Joy had been working in her flower bed and had gloves on. She pulled her gloves off, as she walked toward the hedge. "Miss Love, I'm Joy Fowler. It's a pleasure to meet you."

Now she was standing next to the passenger side of the car. "Did you stay all night, Miss Love?" she asked, as she extended her hand. "I didn't hear you drive in early this morning."

Cassidy started to answer her question, but before she could say anything, Darryl came around the car and faced Miss Joy.

"Yes, she stayed all night, Miss Joy," he said angrily. "Yes, we had sex; and yes, she will probably stay all night again sometime. My sex life does not concern you, Miss Joy. Please keep your nose out of my business. My sex life is none of your business." Then he pushed her toward the hedge, got into the driver's seat and tore out of the driveway and down the road.

"You were a little rough on Miss Joy weren't you, Darryl?" Cassidy asked, a little amused.

"No, I wasn't," he answered still angry. "If anything, I wasn't rough enough. She has had her nose in my business ever since I moved in here and I'm tired of it. Now she wants to control my sex life; that's where I draw the line."

"Is she the reason you wanted me to leave so soon?" Cassidy asked.

"Yes, as a matter of fact she is. I'm sorry about that. I just thought I could avoid a confrontation with her, but it didn't work out," he answered.

They made the rest of the drive in silence. Darryl was still angry and Cassidy was deep in thought. She really didn't like the fact that Darryl wanted to keep their relationship, or beginning of a relationship, a secret.

At the door to her apartment, Darryl took Cassidy into his arms to give her a kiss. "Maybe that's not a good idea, Darryl," she said, as she pushed him away. "I don't think we'll be going out together again."

"Why not?" he asked, his feelings hurt. "Did I do something wrong?"

"You might say that, Darryl," she answered.

"What did I do wrong? You mean because I wanted to avoid Miss Busybody? Is that what you mean?" he asked.

"No, not completely. That might have been part of it, but not all of it," she answered.

"What then?" he asked, not wanting to leave on such a bad note.

"I really don't think we're all that compatible, Darryl," she answered. "We both expected something different from this date. I think I expected too much and you expected too little, bye, Darryl. I'll probably see you at work occasionally. We may even work together sometime, but I don't think I'll go out with you again."

With that, she turned and walked into her apartment and shut the door and left Darryl standing there with a stunned look on his face. It took him a minute to recover. He thought about knocking on the door and trying to get Cassidy to change her mind, but she had hurt his ego and now it would take a while before he would even be able to talk politely to her again. "OK, Miss Cassidy Love," he thought. "If that's the way you want it, then that's the way it'll be. I don't need you. There are too many women who'll go out with me for me to fret over one who won't."

He drove slowly back to his house and into his driveway. Miss Joy was still working in her flower bed and raised her head and watched as he hurried into his house.

"Darryl, you don't know it, but I'm going to make you into the husband that my niece deserves. I know it'll take a lot of time and effort, but I'm determined to do it. You just get ready, big boy, because your time is coming." Then she went back to her gardening.

On Sunday morning, Miss Joy wanted to get Darryl to attend church with her again, but she knew it was too soon after his angry tirade for him to be friendly with her again. She knew he would eventually come around. She already knew that there was something really good deep inside of him that wouldn't let him be angry with her for long. She knew that, as soon as he saw that she needed something, he would give in and apologize and offer to help her. She just had to bide her time until an opportunity presented itself.

When she returned home from church, Darryl was mowing his lawn. She waved at him as she exited her car. He looked right at her, but didn't return the wave. He just turned his back and mowed in the opposite direction.

"OK, Darryl, so you're still mad at me," she thought. "I'll give you a little longer. I think I'll fry a chicken and fix some mashed potatoes and purple hull peas and fried okra. Then I'll invite you over for dinner. They say the way to a man's heart is through his stomach. I think I'll put that to a test and see."

When everything was ready, Miss Joy made her way through the hedge and knocked on Darryl's door. Darryl had been trying to cool off after mowing the lawn, so he was sitting in the den drinking a cold beer. He was wearing a pair of short cut-offs and no shirt. He answered the door carrying his beer because he didn't expect to see Miss Joy and intended to dismiss whoever it was.

"Miss Joy," he said surprised to see her. He held the beer behind his back to hide it from her, but she had already seen it.

"Darryl, you don't have to hide your beer. I've already seen it," she said, as she pushed past him and walked into the room without being invited. "I'm sorry that I made you mad yesterday, but I just didn't know you did that sort of thing."

"What sort of thing is that?" he asked, as he followed her into his den and sat down after she settled herself on his sofa.

"You know what sort of thing I mean," she answered, embarrassed to say the word.

"Miss Joy," he began. "I'm a healthy male; I am a healthy bachelor, a healthy bachelor with healthy, bachelor needs. When I find a lady I would like to fulfill those needs and if she is willing, I will bring her to my house and fulfill those needs. Yes, Miss Joy, I do have S-E-X. Now, if it offends you that I have sex so close to your house, then I apologize to you, but I will continue to have sex with whomever I want to have sex with."

Miss Joy was blushing the whole time Darryl was continuing his tirade. "OK, Darryl, you don't have to be so graphic. I know what you're talking about. I didn't come here to continue our disagreement on how you're supposed to live your life. I came to ask you to come have dinner with me. Will you forgive me and come have dinner with me?"

"I don't know," Darryl answered. "Will you stay out of my sex life?"

"Yes, I will, if you'll come have dinner with me," she answered. "I promise I won't mention your sex life again."

"OK, you go on back over to your house and I'll change clothes and be over in a few minutes."

As Miss Joy made her way back through the hedge and into her house, she had a satisfied smile on her face. "Well, Darryl, you don't know it, but your bachelor days will soon come to an end," she thought to herself.

CHAPTER 6

ON MONDAY MORNING, as Mark sat in his office preparing the procedure for his unit's new assignment, Cassidy knocked on his door. "Can I talk to you for a few minutes, Mark," she asked.

"Sure, come on in, close the door and sit down."

As Cassidy sat down in a chair facing Mark, he put his pen down and leaned back in his chair. "What can I do for you, Cassidy?" he asked.

"I have a personal problem," she started, a little nervous at what she wanted to talk to Mark about.

"If this is about you and Darryl Stevens, I really don't want to get involved," Mark said, before she could continue. "I told you what I thought before you went out with him. I gave you some good, sound advice and you ignored me and went anyway, didn't you?" he asked.

"He's not the innocent boy you thought," she answered. "I didn't use him; he was planning on using me. That's not exactly what I wanted to talk to you about, though."

"What do you want to talk about then?" he asked.

"Do you think I'm sexy?" she asked, just asking him outright.

Mark had a silly grin on his face and hesitated to answer. "What are you trying to pull, Cassidy? You know I could get into a lot of trouble, just by answering that question."

"What we talk about right now won't go any farther than this room, as far as I'm concerned," she said. "I really want to know, do you think I'm sexy?"

"OK," Mark finally answered. "Yes, I think you're sexy. What does that have to do with anything?"

"Then what's wrong with me?" she asked. "Why didn't you ever make a pass at me like every other male does?"

"For one thing, I've always been hung up on Cat ever since I first laid eyes on her. For another thing, you're not my type."

"What's wrong with me, then?" she asked. "Why am I not your type?"

"Look, Cassidy, I don't think this is the proper place for this conversation. Now if you really have a problem, get to it. If not, then get back to your desk and do what I told you to do."

"OK, Mark," Cassidy finally got to the point of her problem. "Why is it that every guy that goes out with me, immediately thinks I'm ready to hop into bed with him? You're a man, you said you think I'm sexy, do you want to go to bed with me?"

"All right, now, Cassidy, you're treading on dangerous ground," Mark said, as he rose from his chair and started to show her the door. "You can get me into a lot of trouble and I could lose my job. Is that what your trying to do?"

"No, Mark," Cassidy said with tears in her eyes. "I really want to know what's wrong with me. The only reason Darryl Stevens asked me out was so he could take me to bed. That really hurt, because I really liked him. I thought we could have something special. Now tell me seriously, what is wrong with me?"

"OK, Cassidy, for starters, it's those clothes you wear," Mark said, as he sat back down behind his desk. "Look at them. Pretend you're a man and look at yourself and tell me what you see."

"I guess you're right. They are pretty revealing," she said, as she looked at her clothes as a man would look at them.

"They're not only revealing, they're advertising," Mark said. "That's another thing. When you look at a man, you look like you're asking him to go to bed with you.

"If you want to know what I think real sexy is, look at Cat. She's sexy as hell and she doesn't have to wear clothes like that. Nor does she invite a man into her bed each time she looks at him. I fell in love with Cat the first time I laid eyes on her and she didn't even know she was sexy. I'm sorry things didn't work out with Darryl like you thought they would, but I tried to tell you. I think you probably advertised falsely. You didn't live up to your claims, I'm guessing."

"I told you, he's not that wide-eyed innocent teenage boy you thought he was. He had everything planned before he picked me up for our date. He gave me a corsage. He ordered wine for our meal. He took me to his house and almost immediately invited me upstairs to his bedroom. I was right when I told you he was a player. I've already crossed him off my list. I just wanted you to tell me what's wrong with me, so I don't let that happen to me again. It hurt, Mark. It really hurt."

Cassidy began to cry and Mark took a couple of tissues from the box on his desk and handed them to her.

"Here, dry your eyes. If he's like you say he is, then he doesn't deserve your tears. Get rid of those clothes and come to work in the morning with proper clothes on. Then see how different the guys treat you. I've offered you some more good advice. Do you intend to follow it or just throw it away like you did the other advice I gave you?"

"Thanks, Mark," Cassidy said, as she dried her eyes and stood to leave. "I think fatherhood has mellowed you some. I can't believe I could have talked to you like this before you became a father."

"You're right, Cassidy," Mark said with a dreamy look on his face. "You can't imagine the feeling I get when I hold one of my kids in my arms or they put those tiny arms around my neck and say, 'I love you, Daddy.' Outside of Cat saying she loves me, it's the second most wonderful feeling I have ever felt in my whole life."

As Cassidy rose to go, Mark said, "Wait a minute Cassidy, before you go. Here's something I wish you would read. This is a tract that my church distributes. It gives you the plan of salvation and tells you how to live your life after you give your life to the Lord. Read it, and if you have any questions, let me know. I'd like to talk to you about your soul, if you'll let me. I wish you'd come over to my house some time and I'll really explain it to you."

"Well, thanks, again, I might just do that," Cassidy said, as she went back to her desk and Mark finished working on his unit's new assignment again. As he worked, he said a prayer that Cassidy would accept the invitation he extended to her to come to his house to talk about her soul.

At lunch time, Mark was sitting at a table in McDonald's, when Darryl walked up to him and asked, "Mark, may I join you?"

"Oh, Darryl, sure, sit down," Mark said, indicating a chair where he should sit.

As they were eating, Darryl said, "Mark, I need to talk to you about something, but not here. I need to talk to you in private."

"Look, Darryl, if this is about you and Cassidy, forget it. I don't want to have anything to do with your problem. Just leave me out of it."

"That's not what I wanted to talk to you about, Mark," Darryl said. "This concerns my unit, not my personal business."

"OK, then," Mark answered. "Come by my office this afternoon and we'll talk."

"Thanks, I'll do that," Darryl said. "By the way, you mentioned Cassidy. Did she say something to you about our date?"

"I told you already that I don't want to get involved in your personal life. I've already gotten more involved than I intended to. Please just leave me out of it. Now, I have to get back to my office. I'm trying to work out a procedure on our new assignment and someone keeps interrupting me. I'll see you later," Mark answered.

"Before you go, Mark, what did Cassidy say?" Darryl continued to try and get Mark to open up to him.

"I told you, I don't want to get involved, so just drop it, Darryl. I'll see you later," Mark said as he walked off.

"Dang, Cassidy must have said something to Mark or he

wouldn't have thought I wanted to talk about her," Darryl said to himself, as he picked up his trash and threw it into the trash bin and followed Mark to the parking lot.

As soon as Darryl could find a minute, he left his office and made his escape to Mark's office. When he knocked on Mark's office door, Mark looked up and motioned for him to enter and sit down.

Darryl walked in and closed the door. "Mark, I have a problem. I hope you can help me solve it."

"OK, Darryl, let's get this over with," Mark answered, as he laid his pen down on his desk. "What can I do to help you?"

"You know I've only been here one week," Darryl started. When Mark nodded his head, Darryl continued. "I wanted to take my time and assess each of my team members and see which one was the most qualified and capable to be my SIC.

"Well, Director Halbert put an end to that. He called me into his office yesterday and told me he wants me to take the two-weeks training at the Academy as soon as possible. I barely had time to even read some of the case files. I have no idea who is even capable of filling in for me the two weeks while I'm gone. Mark, do you know Scott Harding?"

"Yes, I know Scott," Mark answered. "I worked with him when I was Commander of your unit. What about him?"

"Do you think he's capable of filling in as temporary Commander for the two weeks I'll be gone?"

"Scott is a very capable agent," Mark said. "I was proud to have him on my team, but I think you should consider Lee Garrison. Lee is quite capable and he has filled in as Commander many times."

"What do you think of Scott, though?" Darryl was persistent. "I need to know if you think he would be capable of handling the job while I'm gone."

"I told you, Darryl," Mark said angrily. "I think Lee would be a better choice. You wanted my opinion and I gave it. I think that's all I need to say. Is there anything else I can help you with?"

"No, that was what I needed," Darryl said, as he stood and

walked to the door. "One thing more before I go. May I talk to Cassidy for a few minutes? I'll only be a few minutes."

"You can see her for a few minutes, but no longer," Mark said, as he walked to the door to point to Cassidy's desk. "She's busy with something I need, so don't stay too long. That's her desk over there."

As Darryl walked up to Cassidy's desk, she raised her head and looked at him with a frown on her face. "Hello, Cassidy," he said.

"Hi, Darryl," she answered. "I didn't expect to see you this soon."

"I wanted to apologize to you for the other night," he said sheepishly. "I think I misunderstood the reason you went out with me. I guess I don't know as much about what women want as I thought I did."

"You sure had me wrong, Darryl," she said, relaxing a little since he was apologizing.

"I just wondered if you would give me another chance. Let me start all over again," he continued.

"No, Darryl. I don't really think that we have that much in common. I think it would just be a waste of my time and yours, too."

"I could learn to be different, if you just give me another chance," he almost pleaded.

"Darryl, I don't really like you," she finally said. "You're too egotistical and self-centered. I really don't think it would ever work for us. I'm not going to go out with you again, so forget it. Now, I'm very busy. Leave and let me get back to my work."

"OK," Darryl said, as he slowly backed away from her desk. "I think you're making a mistake, though. I think we could have had something, bye."

As he walked out the door, Cassidy followed him with her eyes. She had to brush a tear away, but she was determined not to cry. "I think it was for the best," she thought. "He just wasn't right for me. Maybe some day I'll find the right one; then I'll know it right off. I think I'll try using Mark's advice. Tomorrow, I'll be a different person altogether."

Back in his office, Darryl still had a quandary. Mark had been pretty evasive when he asked him if he thought that Scott would be a good choice for a temporary Commander. Mark had immediately suggested Lee Garrison. Was there some reason that Mark wasn't confident enough in Scott to admit that he would make a good acting Commander? He emphasized the fact that Scott was a good agent, but stopped short of saying that he would make a good SIC even. "What should I do?" Darryl questioned himself. "I certainly don't want to make a mistake this early in my job as Commander."

Then he decided to talk to each of the two men and see if he could get an idea what to do by talking to them. He called Scott into his office first.

"Come in, Scott and shut the door. Have a seat," Darryl said, as Scott appeared at his door. "Tell me why you want to be my SIC."

"Well, isn't that every career agent's goal?" Scott asked. "You know, to become SIC and eventually Unit Commander."

"You did tell me that you had filled in as SIC for Jason Hall, didn't you?" Darryl asked, as he wrote on a tablet on his desk.

"Yes, I did several times. Once when he got married and another time when he was injured. I feel that I can handle the job," Scott said.

"OK, thanks, Scott, I'll let you know," Darryl said. "You can go now. Will you please ask Lee Garrison to stop in here for a few minutes?"

When Lee knocked on the door, Darryl invited him to come in, shut the door and sit down. "Lee, I will be attending the Training Academy for two weeks soon and I need someone to fill in for me while I'm gone. I haven't had a chance to assess the abilities of each of you. I need to know if you've had any experience filling in as SIC or Commander."

"Yes Sir, I've filled in for Mark Fuller several times when he was our UC. That was years ago, though. I haven't filled in recently," Lee answered.

"Do you have someone that you would recommend?" Darryl asked, just to see if he would name himself.

"I think Scott Harding has filled in recently," Lee answered.

"Then would you recommend him?" Darryl asked, writing on his tablet again.

"I'm sorry, Sir, but I don't think it would be good for me to recommend anyone. It might cause bad feelings in the unit and I think that would be bad for the morale. All I can do is say that Scott has filled in recently as SIC," Lee answered.

"Mark Fuller highly recommended you as a fill-in for me while I'm gone for two weeks," Darryl said. "What do you think about that?"

"I appreciate it that Mark feels confident enough in my abilities that he would recommend me, but I have to be honest and tell you that I have never been put to the test. So I can't say how I would do as an acting UC," Lee answered.

"So you don't feel comfortable enough in your ability to say you would do the job?" Darryl asked, disappointed in his answer.

"No, Sir, I'm not," Lee answered, as he shifted uncomfortably in his seat.

"OK, thank you. You may go now," Darryl said, writing in his tablet as Lee stood to leave.

As Lee left, Darryl gave a big sigh. He still didn't know what to do. Mark had highly recommended Lee, but Lee was hesitant to take the position, even on a temporary basis. He wanted to go ahead and let Scott do the job for the two weeks he was gone and see how he worked out, but he was still hesitant to do so. What if he did and Scott didn't work out? "That would really look bad on my record," Darryl thought. "I can't afford to do something wrong so early in my career as UC. It's almost lunch time. I think I'll go to McDonald's and see if Mark's there. Maybe I can get him to tell me why he wouldn't recommend Scott as acting Commander."

Darryl was right, Mark was at the restaurant, but Jason Hall and another person were sitting with him. Darryl was disappointed, but he asked if he could join them anyway.

"Sure, sit down," Mark said. "Darryl, I believe you know Jason Hall. This is Ted Ames. He's the man whose position you've just acquired. Ted, this is our new UC, Darryl Stevens."

Ted and Darryl exchanged greetings, but for some reason Darryl felt uncomfortable meeting the man he was following as Unit Commander. He also thought that he could feel tension between Mark and Ted. It was probably just his imagination, but he knew that he wasn't going to ask Mark about Scott Harding in front of Ted.

"I hate to leave good company, but I really have to get back to work," Mark said, as he stood to leave.

Darryl's heart sank. He really needed to talk to Mark again. "Mark, do you mind if I walk you to your car?" he asked. "I really need to ask you something."

"Sure, Darryl, but you'll have to talk fast, I'm really busy," Mark said, and he kept on walking toward the door.

"Mark, I really need to know for sure if you definitely have something against Scott Harding; I really need to know. I have to make a decision soon. Please, just be honest with me. Is there some reason you wouldn't put him in charge?" Darryl talked as fast as he could because it didn't take Mark long to reach his car.

"Darryl, I've already told you everything I'm going to tell you," Mark answered a little angrily. "You'll just have to make your choice and if it's wrong, suffer the consequences. For me, Scott would be the wrong choice. I told you who my choice would be. Now that's all I'm going to say. You need to do what you feel is best. You have to learn how to make your own decisions and live with the results. That's why you were given the position of UC. If you feel that you're not qualified to make that decision, then maybe you need to resign."

With that, Mark got into the driver's seat and drove off leaving Darryl stunned at the way Mark had just talked to him. Mark was usually nice and cooperative. He seemed like he was already mad, though, before Darryl joined them. Darryl knew he had sensed tension between Mark and Ted Ames. Maybe that was why he had talked to Darryl the way he did.

Darryl looked back toward McDonald's and saw that Jason was still sitting at his table and that Ted Ames was leaving. Jason had also worked with Scott Harding. Maybe he would be more cooperative than Mark had been. Darryl also wanted to know why Jason had refused to take the Commander position of his unit.

As Darryl walked back into the restaurant, Jason rose and started to leave. "Jason, would you wait a few minutes?" Darryl asked, as he caught Jason by the arm and pulled him back toward the table.

"I need to ask you something," Darryl started. "You don't have to answer if you don't want to, but some of the guys in my unit have asked me and I can't answer them. They want to know why you didn't accept the UC position of their unit."

"Well, Darryl, it's like this," Jason said, as he sat back down. "I've worked with those guys for over five years now. We've become like brothers. They think of me as just one of the boys. When I filled in for Ted a few times, I could tell that some of them resented me. They didn't like taking orders from me. I thought about it and figured that if I was given the UC position, it would only get worse. When the other job came open at the same time, I figured it would be best for me to take it and then I could still be friends with my old crew. It has worked out great that way, too. Are you having trouble with them?"

"Yeah, a little," Darryl answered. "They resent the fact that I was given the job instead of you. It would help if you would explain it to them."

"OK, I will," Jason answered, as he started to rise.

"Wait a minute, Jason, I have another problem maybe you can help me with," Darryl said.

"I need to get going, so you'll need to hurry," Jason said, as he sat back down.

"Is there some reason you don't think that Scott Harding would make a good SIC?" Darryl just plunged right in. "I asked Mark about him and he seemed to have something against him, but he wouldn't tell me what it was. Can you tell me?"

"Darryl, if Mark wouldn't tell you, maybe I shouldn't tell you either, but I can see why you need to know. Mark was depending on Scott to have his back, but he let him down. Mark was almost killed. He hasn't trusted Scott since that time. I hope this doesn't turn you against Scott. You just asked why Mark wouldn't recommend Scott and I told you. He may be better now, I don't know. I really have to go now, though."

"Just one more thing, Jason," Darryl said, as they both rose and Darryl followed Jason to the door. "Is there some kind of hard feelings between Mark and Ted Ames? It seemed like I could feel the tension between them and Mark wasn't acting like himself."

"Yes, it all started after Jim Ryan died and Mark was given the UC position. They've been at each other ever since. That's all I can say. It would be best if you don't mention Ted's name to Mark. That's all I've got to say on that subject. Now, I really have to go." Then he got into his car and drove away, leaving Darryl standing in the parking lot wondering what he should do now.

Well, Mark hadn't been much help and Jason hadn't been any more help than Mark had been. Darryl would just have to make his decision on his own. Since Lee Garrison had turned down the opportunity to be acting Commander, Darryl was left with only Scott Harding. "I guess I might as well get it over with," Darryl thought. "I'll have to be leaving on Monday and I need to go over some things with Scott before I leave."

When Darryl got back to his office, he called Scott to come in for a few minutes.

"Scott, I have to make a decision on a temporary Commander because I have to leave for the Academy on Monday. Do you think you can handle it while I'm gone?" Darryl asked, as Scott entered and sat down.

"Yes, Sir, I feel that I can handle it," Scott said. "If you trust me enough to make me Acting Commander for two weeks, I'll do my best to not disappoint you. Is that your decision? Are you giving me the position?"

"Yes, Scott," Darryl said. "I have no other choice. I hope you don't disappoint me. I'm counting on you. Now, I have some things I need to go over with you."

Darryl then spent the rest of the day briefing Scott on anything Darryl thought might arise while he was gone. When Darryl was satisfied that he had given Scott all the information he would need, he finally dismissed him.

Darryl was glad that it was time to go home when he was finished with Scott, because he was exhausted. He had spent a sleepless night tossing and turning last night trying to make a decision. Now that he had finally made his decision, his body was ready to collapse. He could hardly wait until he got home to relax.

When Darryl drove into his driveway, there was an ambulance in Miss Joy's driveway. He quickly parked his car and made his way through the hedge to see what was going on. He didn't know it right then, but it was going to be a long time before he could relax. It was going to be a long, long night.

CHAPTER 7

AS DARRYL APPROACHED the ambulance, he could see the EMT's loading Miss Joy onto a stretcher and starting to put her into the ambulance. "Miss Joy, what happened?" he asked, as he hurried up to her.

She asked the EMT's to wait until she could talk to Darryl. "I fell and they said they think I broke my leg. They're taking me to the Baptist Hospital. Can you come and be with me?"

"Yes, of course, Miss Joy. Where is it?" he asked.

The EMT gave Darryl directions to the hospital and then took off with the lights flashing. Darryl hurried to his car and tried to follow the ambulance.

At the hospital, Miss Joy was taken back to an examination room to be X-rayed and Darryl waited in the waiting room until they told him he could go back and be with her.

"Darryl, I need to call my niece and see if she can come," Miss Joy said. "Can you help me make the call?"

"Sure, Miss Joy, let me see your phone and tell me her name and I'll place the call and then you can talk to her."

"Her name's Tammy Dawson," Miss Joy said weakly. "Can you see her name?"

"Yes, I see it here," Darryl said, as he pushed the icon next to Tammy's name and the phone started ringing. Darryl handed the phone to Miss Joy and let her do the talking. "Hello, Tammy, Dear," Miss Joy said when Tammy answered the call. "Honey, I've done a stupid thing. I fell and broke my leg. Can you come help me for a few months until it heals?"

Darryl couldn't hear what Tammy was saying, but he gathered that she agreed to come. When Miss Joy ended the call, she told Darryl that Tammy had to see if she could get a flight out in the morning and make arrangements to have someone take care of everything while she would be gone. "She said she would call me in the morning and let me know what her flight number was and what time she would arrive. Darryl, I hate to ask you, but would you mind picking her up and bringing her here when she arrives?"

"Miss Joy, I really need to be at work tomorrow," Darryl said, already getting knots in his stomach, again, at the thought of missing his meeting with Scott and going over a few more things with him.

"Maybe you can pick her up and then go on to work after you bring her here," Miss Joy said hopefully.

"Let's wait and see what time her flight arrives and then go from there," he answered.

Then a technician came and got Miss Joy to take her to be X-rayed again. This time she was to have a CAT scan. Darryl waited in the examination room getting more nervous, as the minutes ticked by.

Finally, the technician returned with Miss Joy and she and Darryl waited some more. The hours dragged by until finally the doctor entered holding a tablet computer.

"Miss Fowler, I'm Dr. Lynn Edwards. I'm sorry, but I have some bad news for you. You fractured your tibia. Here, let me show you on this computer." Then he traced the fracture on the screen for Miss Joy. "You'll have to be in a cast for a few months. We're going to have to take you somewhere else to put the cast on. Your friend will have to wait in the waiting room until we finish. You'll be admitted to the hospital and you'll probably be here for a few days. Are you ready to go?"

"Yes, whenever you are," she answered. "Darryl, will you wait and go to my room with me?"

"Sure, Miss Joy," he said. "I'll be here when you get out."

After they wheeled Miss Joy away, Darryl went to the waiting room and got ready for a long wait. He was getting hungry, so he went to the vending machine and selected a drink and some chips. As he sat munching on the chips, he was thinking about his job. Things certainly weren't working out like he thought they would. It seemed as if he had had nothing but trouble right from the beginning. It seemed as if it all started when he moved into the house next door to Miss Joy. Then he was ashamed of himself for blaming Miss Joy for all of his misfortune. He had to leave for the Academy on Monday morning no matter what happened with Miss Joy. Her niece had to get there soon. He had too many other things that would take priority over Miss Joy's problems. The longer he worried over his problems, the more his stomach knotted up. The pain was beginning to be unbearable when Miss Joy's phone rang. Miss Joy's niece's name appeared on the screen, so he decided he needed to answer it.

"Hello," he said hesitantly.

"Hello, who's this?" a sweet-sounding female voice asked.

"This is Darryl Stevens, Miss Joy's neighbor," he said.

"Oh, I thought I got the wrong number when a male answered my aunt's phone," she said. "Where is my aunt, now?"

"They're putting a cast on her leg," Darryl answered. "She asked me to keep her phone in case you called. Did you get a flight for tomorrow?"

"As a matter of fact, I did," she answered. "Will someone pick me up at the airport?"

"I probably will," Darryl said, not too happy at the prospect. "What time will you be arriving and what is your flight number?" he asked.

She gave him her flight information and, just as he ended the call, a nurse wheeled Miss Joy over to where he was sitting and said she was ready to take Miss Fowler up to her room. Darryl ended the call and followed along behind Miss Joy and the nurse. He glanced at his watch and saw it was almost 11:30 p.m.

"Well, I won't get much sleep tonight," he thought. He was right. He drove into his driveway at 2:00 a.m. He staggered up to his bedroom and flopped onto his bed without even taking off his clothes. He was asleep almost before his head touched the pillow. At 7:00 a.m. he awoke with a start, as the morning sun peeped through the blinds on his bedroom window.

"Dang," he said, as he jumped up and pulled off his clothes. "I'm going to be late for work. I have to be on time this morning." Then he jumped into the shower and hurriedly took his shower and dried off and threw on his clothes.

He didn't have time to make coffee, so he drove through McDonald's drive-thru and got a cup of coffee and a sausage biscuit. It was exactly 8:00 a.m. as he pulled into the parking lot. He jumped out of his car and raced toward the building. As he did, he bumped into someone who was racing as fast as he was. He grabbed her shoulders to keep her from falling and, in a surprised voice said, "Cassidy, is that you?"

"Yes, it is," she answered breathlessly. "This is the new me. I decided I needed a new makeover. Do you like it?"

He looked her up and down from the different hair style, to the long maxi skirt and long-sleeved turtle-neck blouse and said, "It's different, but I like it. I would ask you to lunch, but I have to pick someone up at the airport. Can I take a rain check on it?"

"I don't know. I'll let you know later. Right now, I've got to get to the office or Mark will chew me out for being late, bye."

With that, she was gone. Darryl watched her go and whistled to her receding back. "I never thought I'd see that," he said to himself, as he hurried to his office. Scott was already there waiting for him when he arrived.

"Good morning, Scott. I'm sorry I'm late," he said, as he hurried to his desk and pulled out a few files. "I had an emergency last night and I slept late this morning. I'm going to have to leave at noon, too. Do you think you can cover for me for a while this afternoon?"

"Sure, Sir. Just tell me what you want me to do and I'll get it done for you," Scott answered.

They worked in Darryl's office all morning. Then, just before he left, Darryl said, "Here, Scott, while I'm gone, plot this information on this map for me. That'll be our first assignment when I get back from training."

"I'll have it ready when you get back," Scott assured him. "I won't let you down." Then Scott took the information and began to start on it without taking a break for lunch.

At noon, Darryl hurried to the airport to pick up Tammy. Her flight was delayed, so Darryl bought a Coke and a package of chips and munched on them while he waited. He was nervous, and when he was nervous, he ate. Sometimes, he wondered how he kept from weighing a ton, but he worked out at the gym several days a week. If he didn't, he probably would weigh more than he wanted to weigh.

There was only one female passenger on Tammy's flight, so Darryl assumed she was the one. She was fairly attractive. She wasn't gorgeous like Cassidy, but she was pretty enough to make men's heads turn. She had short brown hair with wispy curls accenting her face. She had a slim figure that meant she probably worked out several times a week like he did. He admired her for that. Darryl assumed that she probably watched what she ate, also.

"Are you Tammy Dawson?" he asked, as he walked up to her.

"Yes, are you Darryl?" She answered.

"Yes, I'm Darryl Stevens, your aunt's neighbor. She asked me to pick you up."

"I just have to get my luggage and I'll be ready to go," she answered, as she walked to the luggage carousel. She pointed out her bag and Darryl retrieved it and started toward the exit and expected her to follow.

In the car, he asked if she would like to stop and get something to eat before going to the hospital.

"Yes, that would be nice," she answered. "I haven't eaten since early this morning and I am getting hungry. Just a fast food restaurant will do."

He stopped at a McDonald's close to the hospital and they each ordered a Quarter Pounder and a Coke. They ate quickly and then continued the short trip to the hospital.

In Miss Joy's room, Tammy and Miss Joy exchanged hugs and each one shed a few tears. "How are you feeling?" Tammy asked Miss Joy.

"I guess I could be worse," Miss Joy answered. "I really don't know how, though; I feel like such a fool. Now I won't be able to do anything for a long time. I'm sorry to ask you to come here and take care of me, but I didn't know what else to do."

"That's OK, Aunt Joy," Tammy said, as she patted Miss Joy's hand. "I just graduated from college and I haven't found a job yet, so it's really a good time for me to come."

They visited for a couple of hours and then Darryl asked Tammy if she would like for him to take her to Miss Joy's house.

"I really need to get home," Darryl said. "I can take you to Miss Joy's, if you're ready to go."

"Aunt Joy, is it OK with you if I go on to your house now?" Tammy asked. "If you let me have your keys, I can drive your car back tomorrow morning. If I have your car, I can go and come as I please and I won't have to depend on Darryl to chauffeur me."

"Sure," Miss Joy said. "My keys are in my purse. It's in the locker over there. You can take my purse home with you. I won't be needing it here. I expected you would use my car while you were here. You go on home with Darryl now and I'll see you in the morning."

Darryl dropped Tammy off at Miss Joy's house and carried her suitcase into the house for her. "Do you want to go somewhere for dinner after while?" he asked, as he walked her to the door.

"No, that's OK. I'm sure I can find something in here to eat if I get hungry," she answered. "I'm sure you're tired and ready to go home. Thanks for picking me up and carting me around. I guess I'll see you tomorrow."

"I have to go to work in the morning, but I'll take you to dinner tomorrow night if you'd like to go with me," he answered.

"Sure, I'll see you tomorrow night then," she said. "I think I can find my way back to the hospital."

"Here, I'll write the directions down for you." Then he quickly wrote the directions on a piece of paper and handed it to her. "I need to go now. I'll see you about 7:00 tomorrow night. You'll be home by then, won't you?"

"Yes, I should be home by then," she answered, as she opened the door for him to leave.

Darryl then made his way over to his house. He could hardly wait until he could make it upstairs to his bedroom. He started shedding his clothes on the way up. By the time he reached his bedroom, he was already halfway undressed. He finished undressing and jumped into the shower. He gave a satisfied sigh as the hot water splashed over his exhausted body, revitalizing him and bringing him back to life. He stayed in the shower, letting the hot water massage his tired body for a few minutes, then he reluctantly turned off the water and toweled off.

He needed to get to bed and get some sleep. He had to get to the office early in the morning. There were a few things he needed to do before leaving for two weeks. He still didn't like the idea of being gone for two weeks so soon after just starting his new job, but since the Director had ordered him to, he definitely had to do it.

As he lay on his bed trying to get his weary body to relax enough to go to sleep, he thought about Tammy Dawson. He thought about her slim waist and her full breasts. He wondered how she would feel in his arms. He could imagine the feel of her lips against his own. As he thought of her, he smiled and decided that before she went home, he would know exactly how she would feel in his arms. He would know exactly how those luscious lips felt. He planned to know all about her soon.

CHAPTER 8

DARRYL WAS AT his desk early the next morning. He had accomplished almost half of what he wanted to do before anyone else arrived. When he saw Scott walk by his office door, he called to him. "Scott, when you get settled, I'd like to see you for a few minutes," he said.

When Scott returned, Darryl spent the next couple of hours going over some more information he knew that Scott would need while he was gone. "I really hate to have to be gone so soon after becoming Commander of this unit, but it can't be helped," Darryl said. "I'm depending on you to keep the unit going while I'm gone. You won't let me down will you?"

"No, Sir," Scott promised. "I'll do my best to do everything the way you want it done. I'll try to make you proud of me."

"OK, let's quit and go to lunch," Darryl said. "I think we deserve a rest. Do you want to join me for lunch at McDonald's?"

"Sure," Scott said. So they headed for McDonald's. Mark Fuller was already there when they arrived. "Hello, Mark. May we join you?" Darryl asked.

"Sure, sit down. I could use some company. So you're leaving for the Academy Monday morning, is that right?" Mark asked Darryl.

"Yes, I am," Darryl answered. "Scott, here is going to fill in for me while I'm gone. Do you have any advice for me to make my training go smoothly?" Darryl asked.

"All I can tell you is to do your best," Mark said. "It's pretty intense training. I'm sure you'll get great benefits from it, if you go into it with the right attitude. Just have a positive attitude and you'll do well. Just remember, everyone there wants you to succeed; it's to their advantage if you do well. It gives them more prestige."

"Thanks for the encouragement, Mark," Darryl said. "I'm looking forward to it."

When they finished their lunch, Mark said he needed to get back to the office. "I guess I'll see you when you get back, Darryl," Mark said, then he entered his car and drove back to the office.

"I guess we better get on back to the office, too," Darryl told Scott. "I still have a lot I need to do before I go home this afternoon."

Back at the office, Scott went back to his desk and Darryl finished working on the reports and files that he wanted to finish before he left. At 5:00, he was more than ready to call it quits for the day.

"I'll see you guys in two weeks," Darryl said, as his teammates passed by his office door.

"Sure," they all said. "Hope you enjoy your training."

When he arrived home, Darryl headed upstairs and into the shower. He chose a light blue shirt and navy blue slacks. His hair was wet from the shower, so he dried it with the blow dryer and styled it as he dried it.

It was already after 6:00 by the time he finished grooming, so he hurriedly slipped into his socks and shoes and hurried downstairs. He drove down Miss Joy's driveway and stopped in front of her house. He jumped out of the car and took the stairs two at a time. As he raised his hand to knock on the door, it swung open and Tammy was standing there.

Darryl's heart skipped a beat and he gasped at the pure beauty of the woman standing there. He had been attracted to her when he first saw her at the airport, but this was different. He couldn't take his eyes off of her. Cassidy was gorgeous in a movie star sort of way, but this woman had a clean, wholesome beauty that is so rare. Darryl had never seen such beauty before. He was smitten.

"Are you ready to go?" he asked, when he could finally speak.

"I'll be ready in just a few minutes," she answered, as she stepped back to let him come in. "Come in and sit down for a few minutes."

He watched as she glided up the stairs. It seemed as if her feet didn't even touch the stairs. "She's amazing," he thought. "I'm going to enjoy this."

She was back down in a few minutes. "I'm ready, now," she said, as he stood and grabbed her arm, as she walked past him to the door. He pulled her to him and gave her a passionate kiss.

She put both hands on his muscular chest and pushed away from him. "Aunt Joy warned me about you and your wild parties and womanizing," she said. "Well, you just keep your hands to yourself. I'm not going to be one of your conquests."

He felt like she had just slapped him; it surprised him. He wasn't used to being turned down. "This may be harder than I thought," he thought to himself, as he followed her to the door.

At the car, he opened the door for her and helped her into it. Then he went around and got into the driver's seat. He silently drove to the restaurant. He was still smarting from her rejection. As they were waiting for their food, he relaxed again and decided to get acquainted with her. Maybe she needed to get to know him before going to bed with him, or maybe she was just playing hard to get.

He knew he was good looking. He had been told that many times before. He worked out at the gym several times a week and kept himself in shape, so he knew he looked really good. He was just egotistical enough to think that every woman wanted to go to bed with him the first time she saw him. Boy was he surprised!

"Tell me about yourself," he said, while they waited. "Do you have any brothers or sisters?"

"I have one older brother," she answered. "My mother died when I was very young and my father raised me and my brother alone, so my brother and I are very close. I spent summers with Aunt Joy, so she helped raise me, I guess. She seems like a mother to me, anyway. What about you? Do you have brothers and sisters?"

"I have one older sister," he answered. "She's 10 years older than I am, so she usually bossed me around. She's married and has two children, a boy and a girl. She lives in Florida, close to my parents."

Then the waiter brought their food and they ate in silence.

On the way home, they talked some more about their families and before they knew it, Darryl was driving into the driveway to Miss Joy's house.

"Would you like to come over to my house for a while?" he asked.

"No, thank you. I don't feel like getting into a wrestling match with you tonight," she answered.

"It wouldn't have to be a wrestling match," he said, as he walked her to her door.

"It would be if I went over to your place," she said, as she unlocked the door and walked in. He started to walk in behind her and she stopped him.

"Can't I just come in for a little while?" he asked, still trying to walk into the room.

"No, she said flatly, pushing him back out again.

"Then, don't I deserve a thank-you-for-dinner kiss or a good-night kiss?" he said, as he put his foot in the door.

"OK, just a small thank-you-for-dinner kiss," she said, as she leaned over to give him a small insignificant kiss.

He grabbed her and pulled her to him and gave her an even more passionate kiss than he had before.

She pulled away and gave him a good hard slap on the cheek, "I told you I'm not interested in you," she said, as she pushed him back out the door and shut and locked it.

"That hurt," Darryl thought. "I've never been rejected like that. What's her problem, anyway? Well, there are other fish in the sea. I don't need to keep trying to catch that one."

That night, he tossed and turned wondering why Tammy had rejected him so violently. The next morning, he was determined to find out. He decided to take Tammy to breakfast and then to the hospital. He figured if Miss Joy was going to be released, Tammy would need some help getting Miss Joy home. "What's wrong with that woman, anyway?" he wondered. He had never been rejected by any woman. Why would this one reject him?

When he arrived at Miss Joy's door, Tammy greeted him with a smile. He wasn't expecting a smile, but it was welcome.

"Am I glad to see you," Tammy said, as she took him by the arm and pulled him inside. "They're releasing Aunt Joy this morning and I need some help getting her home and into the house. Will you help me?"

Darryl started to say, "Yes, that's why I'm here," but then he thought he could work it to his advantage. So instead, he said, "What's in it for me?"

"What do you mean?' she asked.

"Like, maybe a kiss without being slapped; that's what I mean," he answered with a grin.

"OK," she said, a little defeat in her voice. "If you help me with Aunt Joy, I'll give you a kiss."

"I don't want just a kiss," he said. "Not a peck on the cheek or a weak, uninteresting kiss. I want a kiss full of passion."

"I'm sorry, but I can't give you a kiss full of passion, because I don't feel passionate toward you. You'll just have to settle for what I give you and be happy about that."

"OK, I'll take what I can get," he said. "I want it in advance, though." Then he took her into his arms and gave her a passionate kiss, anyway. She drew back her hand and started to slap him, but he caught her wrist and stopped her. "Don't go back on our deal already," he said, with an impish grin. "Now, I'll help get Miss Joy home. You've already paid me."

She gave him a withering look and turned to go up the stairs. "I have to get my purse and then I'll be ready to go" she said, as she ran up the stairs and into her bedroom. As she passed the dresser, she caught a glimpse of her face in the mirror. It was bright red. "That man is impossible," she said to herself. "I'll sure have to be on guard around him."

She found her purse and hurried down the stairs and out the door to the car before he could say anything to her. She didn't wait for him to open the door for her. She opened it and was already seated by the time he made it to the driver's seat.

"What's your hurry?" he asked, as he fastened his seat belt and started the engine.

"I thought you might be in a hurry to get back to what you were doing," she lied.

"I have nothing planned for today," he answered. "I'm going to devote the entire day to you and Miss Joy. Now, first, we're going to McDonald's and have breakfast; I'm starving."

She started to protest, but seeing the determined set to his jaw made her stifle what she had intended to say.

They made the stop at McDonald's and then on to the hospital. When they arrived at the hospital, Miss Joy was already chomping at the bit. "Where have you two been?" she asked. "I've been ready for hours."

"It's only 9:00 Aunt Joy," Tammy answered. "They probably won't have your paperwork ready for another two hours. We came as soon as we could."

Tammy was right. The nurse came in and said they would have everything ready for her to go soon, but it was an hour and a half before they came to get her and take her downstairs. They loaded Miss Joy into the front passenger's seat and Tammy crawled into the back seat.

"Do you want to stop at the pharmacy and get your prescriptions filled?" Darryl asked, as he started the engine and began moving forward.

"Yes. I'd like that," Miss Joy said. "Stop at Simmons Drug Store, please."

"Sure," Darryl answered and drove directly to the pharmacy.

"I didn't know you knew the way to the drug store," Tammy said.

"I've been here before," Darryl answered, but he didn't say why he had been there.

Darryl and Miss Joy waited in the car while Tammy went into the pharmacy and filled Miss Joy's prescriptions.

When they arrived at Miss Joy's house, Darryl helped Tammy get Miss Joy into her house and upstairs to her bedroom.

When Darryl and Tammy came back downstairs, he caught Tammy by the arm and said, "You owe me another kiss."

"What do you mean?" she asked pulling her arm out of his grasp.

"I helped you get Miss Joy home," he answered. "Our deal didn't say anything about getting her upstairs to her bedroom. You owe me another kiss for that." Then, before she could say anything, he pulled her into his arms and gave her another passionate kiss.

She started to slap him again, but he grabbed her arm again and stopped her. "Each time I do something for you, like helping you with Miss Joy, you owe me a kiss," he said. "Don't you think I deserve something for my effort?"

"I didn't say I would kiss you again," she said angrily. "I just won't ask you to help anymore."

"OK, just be that way then," he said, as he walked toward the door. "If you need me, you know where I am and what it'll cost you." Then he got into his car and drove over to his house.

Tammy ran to the door and watched as he got out of his car and strutted into his house. "You think you're so smart, Mr. Stevens, but I can help Aunt Joy all by myself. We'll see who gets the last laugh." She could still feel his lips on hers. She touched her lips and thought about how warm his lips felt on hers. If she hadn't known what a womanizer he was, she might enjoy kissing him. She had been taught to stay away from men like him, though. They meant nothing but heartaches.

Aunt Joy had already told her about him. "He's one of those love 'em and leave 'em kind of guys," Aunt Joy had said. Right now he thinks he'll never settle down and get married, but we can change his mind about that. It'll just take time for us to change his mind for him. You need someone who'll marry you and give you a family. We just have to convince Darryl that he's that man. The first thing we have to do is stop his carousing."

She could just hear Aunt Joy now as she told her all of the bad characteristics of Darryl Stevens that would have to be changed.

"Well, it's just as well that she didn't like him. He certainly wasn't what she was looking for, and didn't know if she wanted to try to change him or not. She had saved herself for the man she would marry and she wanted someone who had done the same and it certainly wasn't Darryl Stevens.

"Tammy, can you come help me?" she heard Aunt Joy call. This immediately shook her out of her reverie.

"Yes, Aunt Joy, I'm coming," she answered and hurried up the stairs.

After she got Aunt Joy settled nice and comfortably in bed, she started to go back downstairs.

"Tammy, tomorrow is Sunday," Aunt Joy said. "Do you think Darryl would go with us and help me get in and out of the car and into the church?"

"No, Aunt Joy," she answered too quickly. "No, I don't think he would. He's going out of town Monday and I'm sure he has a lot to do tomorrow."

"Why don't you call and ask him," she insisted. "I'm sure he'll go if you ask him. He's always ready to help me when I need his help."

"No, Aunt Joy," she said again. "I don't want to bother him. You need to stay home tomorrow, anyway. You can go next Sunday."

"I want to go tomorrow," Aunt Joy insisted. "If you don't want to ask him, hand me the phone and I'll ask him."

"OK, Aunt Joy. I'll call him and ask him, but I'm sure he's too busy," she said.

She walked slowly down the stairs. She debated on whether to call Darryl and ask him or to pretend she called and lie to her aunt. She had never lied to Aunt Joy and she didn't want to lie to her now, but she just couldn't call Darryl. If he helped her with Aunt Joy, he would expect her to kiss him again and she didn't think she could make it if he kissed her like that again. After all, there was just so much temptation a girl could stand. She touched her lips with her fingers again and again she could feel his warm lips on hers. How could she ever resist those lips again.

Darryl answered the phone after the first ring. He knew it was Tammy because the caller ID said Miss Joy. "Hello, Tammy," he said, as he answered it. "What can I do for you?"

"Don't be so smug, Darryl Stevens," she said, immediately getting on the defensive. "I'm calling because Aunt Joy wanted me to call, not because I need you."

"OK, what does Aunt Joy want, then?" he asked with a grin.

"She wants to know if you'll go to church with us tomorrow and help her into and out of the car and into the church building," Tammy said.

"I knew you couldn't get along without me," he said laughing.

"No, it isn't me; it's Aunt Joy," she said.

"If I do help you, you'll owe me for each time I help Aunt Joy into or out of the car or church," he said. "Let's see, that'll be four times. So that means four kisses."

"Well, you have to get them from Aunt Joy, because she's the one who wanted your help this time, not me," she said haughtily.

"You're the one I'll collect from or I won't do it," he said knowing she would eventually give in.

On Sunday morning, Darryl was up early. He fixed a pot of coffee and ate a bowl of cold cereal.

At 10:30 a.m., he was knocking on Miss Joy's door. Tammy figured it was Darryl, so she hurried to the door and opened it wide.

"Good morning, Tammy," Darryl said, as he entered the hallway. "How are you this fine morning?"

"I'm great," Tammy said, trying not to stare at Darryl. He was wearing a navy blue suit with a light blue shirt and a red and blue striped tie. He was even more handsome than he had been in jeans and a T-shirt. She caught her breath, as her heart skipped a beat. "Gee, you sure clean up nicely," she said, as he walked past her into the den.

"Thanks. You look nice, too," he said, as he looked her up and down. "Is Miss Joy ready to go?"

"Yes, she is. She stayed upstairs until you came to help her get downstairs and into your car," Tammy answered.

"OK, let's get started," Darryl said and walked toward the stairs. As Tammy walked up behind him, he turned and pulled her to his chest and kissed her.

"What's that for?" she asked in a surprised voice. "You haven't done anything yet."

"I usually take my payment in advance," he said and he started walking up the stairs.

"Good morning, Miss Joy," he said, when he saw her sitting in a wheelchair in her bedroom. "How are you this beautiful morning?"

"I'm not as chipper as you are, that's for sure," she answered. "This thing is going to be the death of me. I can't do anything with this heavy thing on my leg. Thank you for helping."

You're welcome, Miss Joy," Darryl said, as he lifted her out of the wheelchair and handed her a crutch. Here, use this and put your arm around my neck. We'll get you downstairs and into my vehicle in nothing flat," he said.

Tammy was amazed at how easily Darryl handled Aunt Joy. She could see the muscles in his arms flex, as he handled Aunt Joy. She felt ashamed of herself for watching him so intently, but it was so hard to take her eyes off of him. He really had a beautiful body. She wondered what it would look like without his clothes on. Then she really felt ashamed of herself for even thinking such thoughts. "I'll have to really pray for forgiveness when we get to church," she thought. Darryl got Miss Joy comfortably settled in the front passenger's seat, then he loaded her wheelchair into the trunk. He figured it would be more comfortable for her to sit in her wheelchair than to try to sit on one of the pews. It turned out that he was right.

Rev. Baxter preached on sin; not just any sin, but the sin of lust. Then he said lust leads to fornication. Fornication then leads to all sorts of other sins. As he preached, Darryl squirmed in his seat; he was very uncomfortable. He felt that Rev. Baxter was preaching directly to him. "He must have prepared this sermon just for me," Darryl thought. When the sermon was over and everyone filed out and shook Rev Baxter's hand, Darryl could hardly look him in the eye.

"Thanks for bringing Miss Joy to church, Darryl," Rev. Baxter said. "I know how she hates to miss church."

"You're welcome, Rev. Baxter," Darryl said, as he hurried past him and pushed Miss Joy on out to the car as fast as he could.

"Do you want to go to the restaurant and have lunch before you take me home, Darryl?" Miss Joy asked, as Darryl helped her into his car.

"Not really," he answered. "But I'll take you, if you want to go."

"Tammy, do you want to go to the restaurant?" Miss Joy asked.

"If Darryl needs to go on home and get ready to go out of town, I can fix something at home. That way, he can get home and do what he needs to do," Tammy said.

"OK, that settles it; we'll go on home," Miss Joy said.

Darryl breathed a sigh of relief. He wanted to go home and think over what Rev. Baxter had said.

CHAPTER 9

EARLY MONDAY MORNING, Darryl threw his bags into the trunk of his car, locked his door and drove the short distance over to Miss Joy's house. When he knocked on the door, Tammy hurried to answer it. She was surprised to see Darryl standing there.

"I thought you would already be gone by now," she told him, as she stepped aside to let him enter.

"I had to collect my pay before I left," he said grinning. Before she could say anything, he pulled her to his chest and gave her a long, passionate kiss. "That's one," he said. "You owe me three more. I'll collect them when I return. Is there anything you need before I leave?"

"No," she gasped. "I can't think of anything. Aunt Joy wants to stay up in her room today. I think that trip to church yesterday tired her out."

"Well, I'll see you in two weeks, then," he said. "You have my number, if you need me for anything. I don't know how I can help you, since I'll be so far away, but you can call me anyway. I'll call you every now and then to let you know how I'm doing, if that's OK."

"Sure. I'd love for you to call and let us know how you're doing. I know Aunt Joy will really want to know if you're all right."

"Well, I guess I better run," he said then he leaned over and gave her a quick kiss. "That's not one of my kisses that you owe me. That's just a good-bye kiss, just an extra."

Then before she could say anything else, he was out the door. He jumped into his car and was gone.

She watched him until she couldn't see his car any longer, then she sighed and walked up the stairs to Aunt Joy's room. "Well, Darryl's gone," she told her aunt. "He'll be gone for two weeks. We'll just have to make do without him until he returns."

Tammy was surprised when the phone rang at noon and Darryl said, "Hi, Tammy. I made it without having any trouble. Is everything OK there?"

"Yes, Darryl, everything is fine here. I really wasn't expecting to hear from you so soon. I'm glad you made it all right."

"I just got here and already I'm lonesome," he said. "I've already registered and met some of the other unit members. I'm in my room now. It really is a nice room, it just needs a roommate. Too bad you couldn't have come with me."

"I wouldn't have been your roommate, anyway," she answered. "You know that."

"I know, but I can dream, can't I?" he asked, grinning, even though he knew she couldn't see him.

"Don't waste any dreams on me, Darryl," she said, even though her heart skipped a beat at the thought of him dreaming about her.

"Well, I guess I better go and see if I can find out what I'm supposed to do next," he said. "I just wanted you to know I made it safe and sound, as if you really cared. I'll talk to you later. I…"

He started to say I love you, but he caught himself just in time. That would never do. He had never told a woman that he loved her. There were too many traps a man could step into admitting his love for a woman. "Like Rev. Baxter said in his sermon, it's lust, not love. I really do lust after Tammy. Well, I better go see if I can find out what I'm supposed to do," he thought.

Darryl was busy with his training for the next few days and at night, he fell into bed and was sound asleep before his head hardly had time to hit the pillow. By Thursday, though, he was used to the exercise, so he thought he would call and see how Miss Joy was doing.

"Hi, Tammy," he said when she answered the phone on the second ring. "How are things going?"

"Everything here is fine," she answered. "Aunt Joy can get up and down the stairs by using her crutch and putting her arm around my shoulders. She said that my shoulders weren't as nice and big as yours, but they'll do in a pinch."

"I'm glad to know I'm being missed," he said. She could hear a little of the loneliness in his voice. She had a funny feeling in the pit of her stomach when she thought about how lonely he must be feeling. He hardly knew anyone here to begin with and then he had to go over a hundred miles for training where he didn't know anyone either. "I guess he really is very lonely," she thought.

"How's the training going?" she asked.

"They told me it was very intense and they didn't lie," he answered. "I have to tell you, it's really rough. I could have probably done this a lot better 10 years ago. My body wants to rebel against me now. I'll make it, though. I have to make it."

"Well, I wish you luck," she said. She was really sympathizing with him. She could almost imagine how it would be, up against men who were younger and stronger than yourself. She thought about his muscular, trim body and decided it probably wasn't as hard on him as he said it was. He was probably just trying to get sympathy from her.

"I gotta go now," he said. "I'll talk to you later."

The next week went faster than the first week because his body was getting used to the intense training. Finally, it was Friday. The graduation exercises were scheduled for noon. There were hundreds of visitors there to watch their relatives or friends graduate. Darryl was going to get an award for marksmanship. In spite of himself, he was getting excited. He only wished that Tammy could be there to see him get his award.

Right at noon, the speeches began. Darryl and the other award recipients marched up to the stage and awaited their turn to receive their award. Darryl was the last to receive his award, so he was standing at the end of the line.

Suddenly, shots were being fired at the people on the stage. The first man fell and then the second one fell. By the time the shooter reached Darryl, he had been spotted and his gunfire had been returned to him. There was total chaos. Before the gunman fled, he had wounded several people in the audience, also.

Miss Joy had gotten Tammy to help her downstairs to the den so she could watch TV and Tammy had sat down to watch it with her.

Suddenly, the announcer said, "We interrupt this show to bring you some breaking news. A sniper has opened fire on the graduation exercises at the FSC Training Academy in Jonesboro. There have been some fatalities and some have been seriously injured. We know for sure that there are at least four fatalities. No names have been released because the families have not been notified yet."

"No, no, no," Tammy screamed. "That's where Darryl is. He told me he would be getting an award today at noon. What's Mark Fuller's number. I need to call him and see if he knows if Darryl's OK."

The announcer on the TV was continuing to tell how the sniper had opened fire as the trainees were receiving their awards, but Tammy couldn't hear any more. She was busily dialing Mark's telephone number. The line was busy, so she dialed it over and over until Mark answered it.

"Hello," he said breathlessly.

"Mark, thank God I got you," she started as fast as she could. "This is Tammy Dawson, Joy Fowler's niece. Do you know how Darryl is? Was he shot? Is he OK?"

"I can only tell you that he is alive," Mark began. "He's seriously injured, but I don't know how badly. I'm getting a group from our Division and we're heading up there. I'll let you know something when I find out. I have to go now. I'll talk to you later."

Tammy and Miss Joy stayed glued to the TV. The camera showed the aftermath of the assault. There were chairs turned over everywhere. You could see what looked like blood stains everywhere. There were people sitting and staring into space. They were so stunned they couldn't say anything. There were people crying. Ambulances were either taking people to the hospital or were treating minor wounds where the people sat. Tammy watched through tear-dimmed eyes to see if there was any sign of Darryl. She saw none.

Mark and the others arrived at the scene at 5:00 p.m. They had a meeting with the Director of the Training Academy and learned the names of the dead agents. Thankfully, Darryl wasn't among the dead, but Director Henderson said that Darryl was in serious condition. He had several gunshot wounds and had lost a lot of blood.

Mark learned that the four confirmed fatalities were the award winners who had been standing on the stage alongside Darryl. The only reason Darryl was not killed instantly, as the others were, is because the security guards at the Academy were finally able to pinpoint the shooter and had returned fire. This had thrown him off balance, so his aim was off. Even though he wasn't a fatality, Darryl would have a long recovery period.

They found Darryl asleep in his hospital room. There was a large bandage on his head, one on his shoulder and a cast on his leg. There were bags on an IV pole that were infusing life-giving fluids into his battered body. As Mark walked over to his bed, Darryl's eyes fluttered open for a second. Then closed again.

The nurse walked in at that moment. "How is he doing?" Mark asked the nurse.

"You'll have to talk to his doctor," the nurse answered. "I'm not at liberty to say anything."

"Who is his doctor?" Mark asked. "I need to know his condition, so I can report it to his superiors."

"Dr. Grey Randolph is his doctor," the nurse answered.

"May I see him?" Mark asked impatiently.

"I'll tell him you want to see him," the nurse said. "Who are you?"

"I'm Unit Commander Mark Fuller with the FSC. Director Paul Halbert sent me here to check on Commander Stevens' condition. I need to know what his condition is as soon as possible, so I can report it to Director Halbert."

"I'll let Dr. Randolph know you want to talk to him," she said and then she left the room.

Shortly, a tall slim man with a short, black beard entered the room. "I'm Dr. Grey Randolph," he said. "I was told you needed to see me."

"Yes, Dr. Randolph," Mark answered. "I need to know Commander Stevens' condition, so I can give a report to Director Halbert."

"Come down to my office and I'll tell you what I know," Dr. Randolph said, as he walked out the door. Mark followed him and told the others to stay in Darryl's room until he returned.

"OK, Commander Fuller," Dr. Randolph said. "Now we can talk without disturbing Commander Stevens. His head wound isn't as serious as we thought at first. It should heal in a couple of weeks without any side effects. He may lose his memory for a while, but I don't think he has a concussion.

His shoulder is the most serious of his wounds. The bullet tore muscles and shattered bone. He'll probably have to have several surgeries and some intensive therapy to be able to use it again. If he's right handed, he'll need to begin using his left hand. He may have to become left-handed for a while afterwards.

His leg will heal in time and he should be able to walk right again. All of this will take time. If you're his friend, you'll need to encourage him. He has a long way to go to recovery. Now, is there anything else you need to know?"

"No, I think you covered everything pretty well," Mark answered. "When can he be transported? I need to get him closer to home."

"In a few days," Dr. Randolph said. "He's getting a blood

transfusion now, because he lost a lot of blood. He's also getting antibiotics in his IV. We'll see how he's doing by Tuesday. If he seems strong enough, we'll release him. Is there anything else you need to know?"

"No, I guess that's it," Mark answered. "I'll have to go back home, but I'll come back when he's ready to go home."

After Mark left Dr. Randolph's office, he made a call to Director Halbert. "Director Halbert, this is Mark Fuller," he said when the Director answered the phone. "I'm here at the hospital with Commander Stevens. I just talked to Dr. Randolph. He's Commander Stevens' doctor. Here's what Dr. Randolph said. Commander Stevens has a head wound, but it isn't real serious. He doesn't have a concussion. He has a bad wound in his right shoulder that will take months of intensive therapy. He also has a gunshot wound to his right leg. Dr. Randolph seems to think that his shoulder wound will be the most serious of the three wounds. It looks like he'll be out of commission for a long time.

"I'm really sorry to hear that," Director Halbert said. "Tell him that we're sorry that this has happened to him. Tell him I put him on medical leave with pay immediately. All of his medical expenses will be paid for by Worker's Compensation. Tell him not to worry about anything, his job as Commander is safe. We'll get an Acting Commander to lead his unit while he's recuperating, but he'll be able to step right back into his Commander position as soon as the doctor says he's well enough to do so.

"Please assure him that the FSC will be behind him every step of the way during his recovery. Please make certain that he understands that. I know you can relate to how he'll feel, Mark, I know you've been there. Try to encourage him as much as you can. Be sure he knows that you've been there and you came out as good, if not better, than you were before. Make sure he knows that. Has his family been notified?"

"Not yet, Sir," Mark answered. "I wanted to wait until I could see him for myself and find out from the doctor his condition first. Now that I know, I'll call them."

"Give me the names of the men who died and I'll take care of notifying their next of kin," the Director said.

"I'll get them for you," Mark answered and then he ended the call.

As Mark walked back to Darryl's room, he couldn't help but be a little angry at how Director Halbert was taking the news of Darryl's injuries. He still remembered how he was treated during his recovery from almost the same wounds.

His job wasn't held for him until he was ready to go back to work. The Director wasn't even concerned that he would ever be able to return to work. Mark knew that that was all in the past and maybe what he went through had served to make the Director more concerned about his employees. Mark didn't know, but he couldn't help but be a little hurt. He was glad that Director Halbert was concerned about Darryl's injuries, though. He chided himself for feeling peeved and tried to feel more sympathy toward Darryl. Now, he had to call Darryl's family, so he needed to show them that he was concerned about Darryl; they would be expecting it.

When Mark called Darryl's parents' telephone number, his mother answered the phone.

"Mrs. Stevens," Mark started. "My name is Mark Fuller. I'm a Unit Commander for the FSC, where your son, Darryl, works."

"No," she said. "Don't tell me what you're going to say. Please don't say what I think you're going to say." Then she began to cry.

"No, Mrs. Stevens," Mark hurriedly said. "He's not that bad. He's injured and is in the hospital, but he's alive."

"Thank God," she said. "I heard about the shooting on the news. I've been trying to reach someone to find out about Darryl. Tell me, how bad is it?"

"He has several wounds," Mark said, trying to ease her into it. "He has a head wound that will be healed in a couple of weeks. Dr.

Randolph said that it isn't all that bad. He doesn't have a concussion, so that's good."

"OK, now tell me the bad part," she said, already guessing that there must be something worse or Darryl would have called her himself.

"He has a bad shoulder wound that will take extensive therapy after it heals," Mark said casually. "He also has a broken leg."

"He's going to be all right, though, you said," Mrs. Stevens said hopefully.

"Yes. The doctor seems to think that he should be as good as new in a few months." Mark tried to sound more confident than he felt.

"Commander Fuller," she said sternly. "You don't really believe that Darryl will be as good as new, do you?"

"Mrs. Stevens, I'm just telling you what the doctor said. I haven't talked to Darryl yet. He was asleep when I saw him. I just wanted to call you as soon as I talked to the doctor, because I knew you would want to know what the doctor said."

"May I talk to Darryl?" she asked.

"I'm not in his room right now," Mark said. "I'm in the hallway. Let me go into his room and see if he's awake."

When Mark entered his room, Darryl was groggily talking to the other members of the unit. He was drifting in and out of consciousness.

"Darryl," Mark said, as he approached Darryl's bed. "I have your mother on the phone. Can you say something to her?"

Darryl reached for the phone and weakly said, "Hi, Mom."

"Darryl, are you all right?" Mrs. Stevens said and she began to cry again.

"Yes, Mom, I'm OK. Don't worry about me," he said, then the phone fell out of his hand and his eyes closed again.

Mark picked up the phone and started to say something, but Mrs. Stevens kept calling Darryl's name.

"He's asleep again, Mrs. Stevens," Mark said when he was finally able to get her to listen to him. "He's just asleep, because of the pain medication they're giving him, Mrs. Stevens. He'll be OK in a few days."

Mrs. Stevens knew Darryl wouldn't be OK in a few days, but at least she knew he was alive. She felt sorry for the other mothers who wouldn't be able to say the same thing.

"Mark," she said. "Tell Darryl, when he wakes up, that I'll be there as soon as I can get there. I'll get a flight as soon as possible. I'll call you and let you know when I can be there. Will you pick me up at the airport?"

"Mrs. Stevens, Darryl will probably be transferred to a hospital near home in a few days. Why don't you wait until we get him there. It'll probably be best if you wait until then. He may even be able to go home when he's released from this hospital. I'm sure he would rather you wait until he gets home before you come." Mark tried to reason with Mrs. Stevens, even though he knew it was probably a waste of his breath.

"I want to be there with him," she said. "I'm coming as soon as I can get there."

"Mrs. Stevens, it would really be best if you wait until he's transferred, anyway." Mark tried again to reason with her. He really hated to have to try to keep up with her while Darryl was in a hospital so far from home. "I'll keep a good watch on him while he's here. Why don't you wait until he leaves this hospital in a few days. I'll call you every day and let you know how he's doing."

"I really need to be with him right now," she said, but she was beginning to give in.

"Right now he's sleeping a lot and you wouldn't be able to talk to him, anyway," Mark thought he would coax her a little bit more. "When he's better, he'll be transferred, then you can come and you'll be able to visit with him while he recuperates.

"Mrs. Stevens, it's 10:00 now and I'm going to go to the hotel for the night, but I'll be here the first thing in the morning to check on Darryl. If he feels like talking, I'll call you and let you talk to him.

I've got to go now. Darryl's asleep and I figure he'll sleep all night. He has some very good nurses. I'm sure they'll take good care of him tonight. I'll talk to you in the morning; good night."

Then Mark ended the call before Mrs. Stevens could say anything else. It had been a long day and Mark was anxious to get to the hotel and call Cat. He knew she would be anxious to hear from him. He was anxious to hear her voice, too.

Then he remembered that he had promised Tammy that he would call her and let her know how Darryl was doing, so he took a few minutes to call her. "Tammy, this is Mark Fuller. I told you I'd let you know how Darryl's doing. He isn't as bad as we thought. He has a head injury that isn't too bad, a shoulder wound and a leg wound. He's doing pretty good, though. I'll have him call you, when he's awake. Gotta go now, bye."

He ended the call before Tammy could ask any questions. He was too tired to get into a long discussion with her. She would just have to wait until he had more time to talk.

CHAPTER 10

MARK AND THREE others from different units had come to the Training Academy. Mark was supposed to see to the care of Darryl Stevens and the others were to see what they could do toward bringing the Academy back into calm again.

Dave Hightower from Mark's unit was one of the other agents who came with Mark. The others were Unit Commander Jason Hall and Bill Williams from Darryl's unit.

They were all up early and went down to the hotel restaurant and ate breakfast before starting another long day. Mark was going to the hospital to check on Darryl and the others were going back to the Academy to see what they could do to bring order there and help the police in their investigation. This was personal to them. They each knew and liked the agents who were killed. They had all been new young recruits: Tim Evans, Kyle Norris, Devin Watts and Craig Eason. They had all won awards, that's why they had been on the stage. They would have been great agents. Their deaths had been a great loss to the Commission.

When Mark walked into Darryl's hospital room, he was sitting up trying to eat a soft breakfast. He was having a hard time using his left hand. He was dropping more on himself than he was getting into his mouth.

"Good morning, Darryl," Mark said, as he walked over to his bed. "Do you need some help there?"

"I guess I could use a little, but I guess I need to learn how to do it myself," Darryl answered. "The doctor said I would be like this for quite some time."

"Here, let me have that fork," Mark said, as he took the fork from Darryl. "You can learn to use your left hand later, but now you need to get some food into you."

Then Mark sat on the side of the bed and fed Darryl until his plate was empty. "You make me feel like a baby," Darryl complained. "Thank you, anyway."

"How do you feel today?" Mark asked.

"I feel like I've been used for target practice," Darryl answered. "I hurt all over. What does the other guy look like?"

"I don't know," Mark said, getting serious. "We haven't caught him yet."

"What about the others?" Darryl asked. "I heard shots and the guys before me fell before I was hit. Are they OK?"

"I'm sorry, Darryl," Mark said, as he bowed his head. "They didn't make it."

Darryl tried to swallow, but couldn't because of the large lump in his throat. "I hate to hear that, they were so young. They would have made good agents. Do you have any idea why the guy did that?"

"No, Darryl," Mark answered. "I'm sorry, but we don't have a clue why or who did it."

"Would you turn on the news?" Darryl asked. "I want to see if they have it on the news."

"I'm sure it's on the news, but I don't think you want to see it, Darryl," Mark answered.

"I need to see it to believe that it really happened," Darryl said. "Right now, it seems like a bad dream. I really need to see it, Mark. Would you turn it on?"

"OK, Darryl, but I don't think you need to see it," Mark said, as he turned the TV set on and flipped through the channels until he found the news about the shooting.

Darryl watched through tear-dimmed eyes for a few minutes, then he started sobbing. "Turn it off, Mark, you're right, I can't watch it any longer."

Mark turned off the TV and sat quietly until Darryl was calm again. "I talked to your mother last night," Mark said. "She wants to talk to you, if you feel like it."

"I don't really feel like it, but I guess I need to. She won't rest until she hears my voice and knows I'm OK," Darryl said. "Would you call her for me?"

"Sure," Mark said, as he dialed Mrs. Stevens' number and handed the phone to Darryl.

"Hello, Mom," Darryl said. "Mom, don't cry, I'm OK. Yes, Mom, I'm OK. No, don't come, Mom, I'll be OK. I have Mark and some others. No, Mom, you need to stay at home and take care of Dad. No, Mom, don't come, I'll be OK. Please, Mom, don't come."

"I can't talk any longer, Mom, I have to go now. Do you want to talk to Mark? OK, here's Mark. Bye for now. I love you. Please don't come.

Mark took the phone and said, "Hello, Mrs. Stevens."

"How is Darryl really doing this morning?" she asked with tears in her voice.

"He's better, Mrs. Stevens," Mark answered. "He's sitting up and he ate a good breakfast. He's awake and talking to me. He's really doing a lot better this morning."

"Let me know when he'll be transferred," she said. "I want to come as soon as he gets home."

"I'll let you know, Mrs. Stevens," Mark said. "I need to go now. The nurse just walked in. Goodbye, Mrs. Stevens." Then Mark ended the call without letting Mrs. Stevens get started again.

"Good morning, Commander Stevens," the nurse said. "I see you ate all of your breakfast. You're doing good this morning. How is your pain level this morning?"

"I guess it's about eight or nine," Darryl said. "I could use some pain meds."

"Sure," she said. "I'll get something for you."

She went out of the room, but was back again shortly with her medicine cart. She removed a syringe from the cart, scanned it and scanned Darryl's wrist band, then injected it into his IV.

"I'm sorry, Mark, but I'm going to leave you now," Darryl said, as his eyes closed.

"That's OK, Darryl," Mark said. I need to go to the Academy for a while, anyway.

At the Academy, Mark talked to Director Henderson, "Have you found out anything about the shooter yet?" Mark asked.

"I don't know anything yet, Commander Fuller," the Director said. "The police were here for hours collecting evidence, but they haven't told me anything yet. The agents you brought with you have gone over everything again now that the police have gone. I haven't talked to them yet. I don't know what they've found, if anything."

"Where are my men now?" Mark asked.

"I think they went into the cafeteria for lunch. Would you like to go have lunch with them?"

"Sure, I'll go see if I can find them," Mark answered. "Are you coming?"

"No, not right now," Director Henderson answered. "I have something I need to take care of right now. I'll be along after while."

Mark remembered the way to the cafeteria from when he attended his training, so he made his way there and found his men.

"Hey, guys, how's it going," Mark asked, as he walked over to their table.

"Hey, Mark, come join us," they said together.

"Let me get a cup of coffee and I'll be right over," Mark answered, heading toward the coffee maker.

When Mark sat down at the table, he asked, "Have you found out anything yet?"

"No. We haven't found out a thing," Jason answered. "The

detectives, who were here, were very closemouthed. They wouldn't tell us anything. I thought that the police usually were cooperative with our agency. These guys acted like they thought we were trying to take their jobs away from them."

"Maybe it's because we're too involved in it," Mark answered. "After I feel that they've had time to process what they have, I'll talk to the Police Commissioner and see what I can find out. I think it's best if I handle it that way."

"If you don't need us here anymore, then, I guess we need to get on back to our units," Jason said. "This is going to be a big blow to each unit. They'll eventually have to be replaced. The units to which they belonged will be short until they are replaced. I think some of us will need to attend their funerals, too. So if we're through here, we need to get on back."

"You, guys can go ahead and go on back," Mark said. "I need to stay here with Darryl until he's transferred."

"How will you get home, if we leave you, Mark?" Jason asked.

"I'm sure Darryl's car is here and it has to be taken back home," Mark answered. "I'll drive it home."

"OK, then, after we eat, we'll load up and take off," Jason said. "Will you take care of the hotel bill?"

"Yes, I have the Director's permission to charge it to FSC. Don't worry about it. You guys go on home and I'll see you when I get back."

Mark went back to the hotel and checked them out. Then he watched as they drove off without him. He had a sinking feeling in the pit of his stomach. He felt as if he had been left on a deserted island and his ship was sailing away without him. He went into his hotel room and called Cat. Suddenly, he had to talk to her. He just had to hear her voice.

CHAPTER 11

MARK WENT BACK to the Academy and talked to Director Henderson again. Things were calming down and the Director said that training would begin again on Monday. Mark thought that was probably too soon, but maybe it was best to get back into the normal routine as soon as possible. Since the next day was Sunday, the Academy would be closed until Monday, so Mark went back to the hospital to check on Darryl.

It was about 6:00 p.m. when Mark walked into Darryl's room. He was again trying to eat with his left hand. "Do you need me to help you again?" Mark asked.

"No, that's OK, Mark," Darryl said. "I need to learn how to do this myself. It looks like I'll be eating left-handed for a long time."

"Since tomorrow's Sunday," Mark said. "I'm going to find a Baptist Church to attend in the morning. I don't like to miss church if I can keep from it. I'll be back to check on you after church. Is there anything I can do for you before I go back to the hotel?"

"No, Mark," Darryl said. "I'll just lie here and try to get better. You look exhausted. Go on back to the hotel and try to rest, I'll be OK. I'll be looking for you tomorrow after church, though. I get lonesome when I'm not asleep."

"I'll be back tomorrow," Mark said. "Do you want me to stay a little longer tonight?"

"That's OK, Mark. You need to go on back to the hotel and rest. I'll be OK tonight. It's almost time for some pain meds. I'll go to sleep when I get that anyway."

"OK, I'll go on then," Mark said, as he walked toward the door. "I'll see you tomorrow."

At the hotel, Mark pulled his shoes off, stretched out on the bed and called Cat. "Hi, Honey, how's everything at home?" he asked.

"Everything's fine," Cat answered. "We just miss you. Do you know when you'll be home?"

"Darryl's doing better today," Mark answered. "He's been trying to feed himself with his left hand. It reminds me of myself when I was in his shape. I guess I can sympathize with him more than the other guys, since I've been through almost the same thing he's going through."

"But you had me to help you," Cat said. "Does he have someone here to take care of him?"

"His mother's coming as soon as he gets home," Mark answered. "He tried to talk her out of it, but she's determined to come. I guess mothers are like that."

"Yes, they are," Cat answered. "No matter how old your child is, he's still your baby. Just wait until ours grow up and see how protective of them I still am."

"I'm going to find a church in the morning," Mark said. "I'm sure there's one somewhere around here close by. I can look in the phone book, I think, and find one close enough that I can walk to it. I don't have a car, since the other guys have already gone home. I plan on driving Darryl's car home when he's released from the hospital, but I don't want to ask him to let me use it for anything else.

"I guess I'll go now and get a shower and go to bed. I didn't get much sleep last night."

"I love you, Mark," she said "Be careful. Remember the shooter may still be around and he must be trying to kill FSC agents."

"I'll be careful, Honey," he answered. He liked how she always showed such care for him now. It made him feel good to know that she loved him as much as he loved her. "Good night, Honey."

"Good night, Mark, take care," she said and ended the call.

Mark was up early the next morning. He found the address of a Baptist Church nearby. He ate breakfast and set out to find the church. When he walked in, he was greeted by several members of the church. They introduced him to the pastor, Dale Green, and several other members. They all welcomed him and told him how glad they were to have him attend their services. Mark felt like he was back in his home church. Some of the members even invited him to eat lunch with them. He declined and said that he needed to go on to the hospital and check on Darryl.

At the hospital, Darryl was trying to eat with his left hand again. "Hey, Mark, am I glad to see you," Darryl said when Mark walked in. "I think I'm going to give up for a while and let you help me. I made a mess of my breakfast, but I'll let you help me with my lunch, if you will."

"Sure, Darryl," Mark answered, as he washed his hands and started to feed Darryl.

Dr. Randolph came into Darryl's room and asked him if he was ready to be transferred on Monday.

"I'm more than ready," Darryl answered. "I'm sure Mark's ready to get back home and he's the one who'll take me."

"OK, Commander Stevens, let us take some more X-rays and if everything looks OK, we'll discharge you to go home. I'll release you to a doctor in your hometown. Then when he feels you're ready, he can set you up with a therapy schedule. How does that sound?" Dr. Randolph asked.

"That sounds great," Darryl answered.

"The nurse will be here soon to take you to X-ray. When I get them, I'll check to see how everything looks and let you know," Dr. Randolph said.

After about an hour, Dr. Randolph returned carrying a computer. "Well, Commander Stevens. It looks like everything's still in place.

If you really want to leave our good company, I'll discharge you in the morning."

"I hate to leave such good company, but I want to get back to my home," Darryl said. "The sooner I get home, the sooner I'll get well and be able to help find the S.O.B. who did this."

"Just remember that you're not well," Dr. Randolph said. "You have a long way to go before you can go back to work. If you don't let your body heal at its own pace, you may not get a healed body. You need to take it easy for a while."

"I understand that, Doc," Darryl said. "But I need to get back as soon as I can."

"Just remember what I said," Dr. Randolph said. "Commander Fuller, I would appreciate it if you'd keep an eye on him for me. Make sure he doesn't do something before he should."

"I'll do my best, Dr. Randolph," Mark answered, but he could remember how anxious he was to get back to work and he knew Darryl would be the same way.

On the way home, Mark had a strong urge to ask Darryl about his standing with God. He would start to ask him and then he would stop. He knew he should ask him, but he was a little hesitant to ask. He and Skip, his brother-in-law, were still conducting the Bible study at the prison and he had no problem asking the prisoners if they were saved. Somehow, though, he just couldn't seem to ask Darryl. Mark knew that Darryl had come to church with Miss Joy, but he also remembered the wild party he had had when he first got there. There had also been alcoholic beverages at that party.

Darryl had also had a fling with Cassidy, who called him a player. This wasn't the kind of behavior that you associated with someone who was a Christian. Mark wondered why he was so hesitant to talk to Darryl about his soul. The three-hour drive home would be an excellent time to talk to him, but Mark just couldn't find the words to ask him. Soon, Darryl lay his head back on the headrest and was asleep. Mark had missed his chance.

When they got to Brinkley, Mark stopped at the Shell Station to fill the car with gas and rest for a few minutes. He was beginning to get hungry. There was a nice-looking McDonald's Restaurant across the street, but he wanted something more than a hamburger. He asked the station attendant if there was a good restaurant around close by and he said, "I recommend Gene's Barbecue Restaurant, it's just down the street. They have good food and friendly people and the prices are reasonable." So Mark asked Darryl if he would like to go there.

"I guess, but I don't know how I'll do eating with my left hand," Darryl answered, as he held his right arm up to remind Mark of his injury.

"We'll try it, anyway, even if I have to feed you," Mark said.

The waitress said that they had a lunch special that included chicken- fried steak with white gravy, mashed potatoes, green beans, a roll and blackberry cobbler for dessert. Mark's mouth started to water and he said, "I'll have that."

"I guess I'll try that, too," Darryl said.

When their food came, Mark cut Darryl's meat up for him and helped him eat. He was able to do pretty good with Mark's help.

After they ate, they hit the road again. Arriving at Darryl's house, Mark helped him to the house and over to the sofa in the den. Then Mark unloaded Darryl's bags. "Do you have someone to stay with you until your mother gets here?" Mark asked.

"No, I guess I don't have," Darryl answered. Then there was a knock on the door. When Mark opened it, Tammy was standing there. "I saw you bring Darryl home," she said. "May I see him?"

"Sure, come on in," Mark said, opening the door wider to allow her to come into the room. "He's in the den."

"Hi, Darryl," she said, as she walked into the den. "How are you feeling?"

"Hi, Tammy," he answered. "Right now, I feel like someone used me for target practice. I had a rough ride home. How are things with you and Miss Joy?"

"Looks like we're better than you," she answered. "Aunt Joy wants to know if you have someone to help you."

"My mother will be here some time tomorrow, won't she, Mark?" Darryl answered.

"Her plane lands at 2:15 tomorrow afternoon and I'll go pick her up and bring her here," Mark answered.

"I don't have anyone until then," Darryl said.

"Why don't you come over to Aunt Joy's until your mother gets here and I can take care of both of you?" Tammy asked.

"Thank you for the offer, but I think I'll be more comfortable here. My mother will be here tomorrow. She'll take really good care of me then. I can take care of myself, if you or Mark will stop by every now and then to check on me," Darryl said.

"Sure, I'll be happy to come over and check on you," she said. "I could do a better job, though, if you were over at Aunt Joy's house."

"I can stop and check on you when I go to work in the morning," Mark said. "That is, if I don't have to go out of town on an assignment. You know how that is, I'm sure."

"Yeah, I know how that is, Mark," Darryl said. "I'd appreciate anything you can do for me, anyway."

"Well, I have to go," Mark said, as he headed toward the door. "Cat's picking me up. She should be here in a few minutes. Yes, there she is now. I'll leave you in Tammy's capable hands. Bye you two."

"Goodbye, Mark, see you later, thanks for everything you've done for me," Darryl said.

"Bye, Mark, I'll see you to the door," Tammy said, as she walked beside Mark to the door. "Mark, before you leave, I need to know something. Is he going to be all right? I know he has a long way to go, but will he eventually be back to his old self?"

"Well, I can tell you this, Tammy, I was right there where he is now and I recovered. It took a lot of love and patience from Cat, but I made it. I'm sure it'll take the same thing to help Darryl recuperate. See you later."

Tammy walked back over to the sofa in the den to find Darryl asleep. He looked so innocent lying there in sleep, that she bent over and kissed him on the forehead. He immediately opened his eyes and grabbed her.

"It was just me, Darryl," she said in a startled voice. "You're OK."

"I'm sorry, Tammy, I guess I still haven't gotten over the shock of the gunshots yet," he said. Then, instead of letting go of her, he pulled her to him and kissed her on the lips. "If you're going to kiss me, then do it right." Then he kissed her again a little harder.

She pulled away from him and said, "I didn't intend to arouse you. I just couldn't resist kissing your forehead. You looked so much like a hurt little boy. I don't think you're as bad off as you're pretending to be. Let go of me."

"I apologize," he said, as he let go of her hand. "I guess it was just a normal reaction. It was pretty nice, though. Can I do it again?"

"No," she said firmly. "I need to go check on Aunt Joy now. I'll come back and check on you later. Do you need anything before I go?"

"Yeah, I do," he said with a wink, but I'm in no shape for it right now."

She blushed and turned and walked out the door, leaving Darryl chuckling on the sofa. Soon, he was asleep again.

CHAPTER 12

MARK SAT IN the airport waiting for Mrs. Stevens' flight to arrive. As he waited, he watched the people come and go. He had been trained to watch for suspicious behavior in people, so he was practicing on the people in the airport. One man in particular caught his eye. He wrote down a description of the man and kept an eye on him. Mark watched as the man drank a cup of coffee and threw the empty Styrofoam cup into a trash barrel, then Mark nonchalantly walked over to the trash barrel and retrieved the cup. He had an empty Wal-Mart bag in his pocket, so he put the cup into the bag and put the bag into his pocket.

Just then the announcement for the arrival of Mrs. Stevens' flight came over the intercom system and Mark lost track of the suspicious person.

"Hello, Mrs. Stevens," Mark said, as he walked up to a lady that he thought would be Darryl's mother. She was short, about 5'2" tall with gray hair, cut short in a becoming cut, a little plump, but not too plump and she looked like Darryl. "I'm Mark Fuller," he said, extending his hand.

"Hello, Mark," she answered, as she took his hand into both of hers in a warm greeting. "I appreciate your taking time out of your busy schedule to come pick me up. How is Darryl doing?"

"The trip home was rough on him, but he's doing better this

morning," Mark answered. "You'll find that he sleeps a lot. You may have to wean him off of the pain medication. I know he's in a lot of pain, I've been there. I know how it is, but he needs to start thinking about therapy. He'll never be able to use his right arm again, if he lets it get stiff. Where do we get your bags?"

"Right over here," Mrs. Stevens said, as she led Mark over to the baggage carousel. "I guess I'm the wrong person to wean him off of pain medication. I can't stand to see him in pain. He's my youngest, you know. I've always been too protective of him."

All the way to Darryl's house, Mrs. Stevens told Mark about things that Darryl had done as a boy. Mark had to laugh at some of the antics that Darryl had pulled as a boy. He would probably be angry at his mother if he knew she was telling Mark some of the things he had done. Mark knew he would be embarrassed, anyway.

Soon, they were pulling up into Darryl's driveway. Mark opened the car door and helped Mrs. Stevens out and then he unloaded her bags from the trunk.

Inside, Mrs. Stevens ran to the sofa and hugged Darryl. When she saw all of his bandages, she began to cry.

"I'm OK, Mom," Darryl said, trying to free himself from her grasp. "It's not as bad as it looks. I'll be as good as new in a few weeks."

Mark brought Mrs. Stevens' luggage into the room and asked, "Where do you want me to put her bags, Darryl?"

"She can have the second bedroom upstairs," Darryl answered. "The first room is my bedroom. I plan on going back up there as soon as I'm able to tackle the stairs."

"Darryl, is there anything else I can do for you or your mother, now?" Mark asked.

"No, I think you've done enough," Darryl answered. "Thanks for everything. Mom can take over now."

"I'll go, then," Mark answered. "My unit's going back up to Jonesboro in the morning to see if there's anything we can do to help find the shooter. I need to get home and get ready to go in the morning. Call if you need me."

With that, he was gone and Darryl was left with his mother as his caregiver. He told his mother everything he could remember about what the doctor told him before he left the hospital.

"When my shoulder and leg heal a little more, I'll have to go for therapy. Right now, Dr. Randolph gave me some exercises to do while I have to stay in bed," Darryl said. "There's some papers there on the coffee table that give some more instructions."

After Mark left, there was a knock on the door. Mrs. Stevens opened the door to find Tammy Dawson standing there.

"Hello, I'm Tammy Dawson," she said. "I'm Miss Joy Fowler's niece. I'm staying with my aunt next door. You must be Darryl's mother. I just came to check on him. How is he doing?"

"My, you don't let a body get a word in edgewise, do you, Tammy?" Mrs. Stevens said. "Yes, I'm Darryl's mother, come on in. I guess you know where to find him."

"Yes, Ma'am, I do," Tammy said, as she walked past Mrs. Stevens and into the den where Darryl was lying.

"Hi, Darryl," Tammy said to him. "How are you doing today?"

"I'm better today." Darryl answered, hoping that his mother believed him. "Mother, this is Tammy Dawson, she's my neighbor's niece. She's been checking in on me to make sure I'm OK. When you go home, she'll probably take care of me. So, you won't have to worry about me," Darryl hoped that his mother would take the hint. All he needed was a mother hen hovering over him. It was bad enough that he was wounded before he could even start his new job. Now he had to be cared for by an overprotective mother. "Would things ever go right for him?" he wondered.

CHAPTER 13

CAT WAS DOING laundry so Mark would have plenty of clean clothes to take with him to Jonesboro. She always went through his pockets, because he usually left something in them that didn't need to go through the wash. There, of course, was something in a pair of slacks that she was examining. When she pulled it out, she was confused. It was a Styrofoam cup in a plastic storage bag.

"Mark," she called. He was in the bedroom packing his suitcase when he heard her call him. He hurried down the stairs and called out, "Cat, where are you?"

"I'm in the laundry room," Cat said, as she walked out to meet Mark.

"What is it, Honey?" Mark asked.

"What is this?" Cat asked, holding up the cup.

"Oh, I forgot about that," Mark said, reaching for it. "You didn't touch it did you?"

"No, I didn't," Cat nervously answered. "Why?"

"There was a suspicious character at the airport when I went to pick up Mrs. Stevens. He was drinking from that cup. I thought I would send it to the lab and find out who he is."

"Well, here, you better take it and put it somewhere before I throw it away," Cat answered.

Mark took the cup and put it on the top shelf of the bookcase in the den. "I don't have time to fool with it now," he said. "I'll take care of it when I get back from Jonesboro. I need to get ready to go now." Mark had put the Styrofoam cup into the bookcase and there it sat, forgotten, again.

"How long before my clothes are ready to go?" he asked.

"It'll be a couple more hours, anyway," Cat answered. "They have to go through the washer and dryer. Then I need to iron your shirts, if you want them ironed."

"That's OK, you don't need to iron them. Just get them washed and dried so I can go. The rest of my team is probably already down at the office ready to go. I need to call and find out," Mark said, as he walked into the den to make his call.

Mark found out that most of his team hadn't made it yet. They were under the impression that the unit wouldn't leave until the next morning. Mark had just expected them to all meet at the barracks that night and be ready to leave from there in the morning. "I guess you'll have time to get my clothes ready," he told Cat. "I won't need to leave until in the morning, I guess."

The next morning, Mark was up at 5:00 getting ready to go. He told Cat to stay in bed. "I'll just grab some coffee and something quick at the cafeteria when I get to the barracks," Mark said. "Hopefully, everyone will be there and be ready to go."

He kissed Cat and went into the rooms of his son and daughter and kissed them. They never even stirred from their sleep. He looked at them with longing eyes. They both looked so innocent. He hoped that they would stay that way, but he knew that, as they grew older, they would try things that he didn't approve of, but he also knew that that was human nature. He just hoped that he would be a good example for them and maybe they wouldn't stray too far away when they were grown.

Mark gave a deep sigh and turned and hurried out of the room. He gave Cat another kiss and held her for a few minutes. "I'll call you when I get a chance," he said, and then he was gone.

Cat ran to the window and watched him as he drove out of the driveway. She said a prayer for him. She prayed for him to have a safe trip there and back. She also prayed that they would be able to find the person who had killed the other agents and wounded Darryl. "I'll have to go check on Darryl while Mark's gone," Cat thought. "That's the least I can do to help."

When Mark arrived at the barracks, almost everyone was already there. He thought that, since he had to wait for the others, he would get a cup of coffee while he waited. When he looked at his Styrofoam cup, he was reminded of the cup he had put in the bookcase at home. "I need to have that checked out when I get home," he thought. Then he made a mental note to take care of it when he got back home.

The trip to Jonesboro was long and boring. Mark hoped that they weren't making the trip for nothing. He hoped that his unit could help find the person responsible for the deaths of four of the FSC agents and the wounding of Darryl.

In his mind, he was forming a plan of procedure. He had used this procedure before, but he had been totally in charge then. Now, he would have to do as the police detective instructed him to do. He really didn't like that, but he knew he had to abide by their rules. It was a sticky situation. The crime had occurred on FSC property, but it was within the jurisdiction of the city police. Both law agencies had to cooperate. He knew he had to go along with whatever the police department dictated, whether he liked it or not.

When Mark and his unit arrived at police headquarters in Jonesboro, they learned that the funeral for Tim Evans was to be that afternoon. The Chief of Police, Douglas Blevins, told them that the family requested that some of the FSC agents attend and be a part of the ceremony. Mark said, "My men and I will be honored to attend and do whatever the family would like for us to do."

At 2:00, the time of Tim's funeral, Mark and all of his men lined up by Tim's casket, looking sharp and handsome in their matching suits and ties. After the funeral, they all shook hands with each member of Tim's family and offered their condolences.

While Mark and his men were in Jonesboro, they attended

the funerals for Kyle Norris, Devin Watts and Craig Eason. At each funeral, they lined up respectfully by the casket wearing their matching suits and ties and offered the family their condolences. Each family member was grateful that the FSC had been represented at their loved one's funeral.

After the funerals, Mark and his team were able to concentrate on aiding the police in their investigation of the Academy shooting. The police had recovered every one of the casings that had been fired and the bullets that had been removed from each of the victims, but there were no fingerprints on any of them.

Mark and his crew spent several days searching the woods where the gunman had been sitting, but turned up no clues.

It was determined that the shooter must be someone who had a grudge against the FSC or the Academy. Another suggestion was that maybe the shooter was targeting only one of the agents and shot the rest of them to put the police off on the wrong trail. Mark and his crew spent two weeks going through files of criminals who had been arrested because of the FSC, but there was not even one who could definitely be pointed out to be the shooter.

Finally, after three weeks of investigating, Mark and his team returned home, disappointed that they were unable to find a suspect in the shooting at the Academy.

CHAPTER 14

WHILE MARK AND his unit were in Jonesboro, Darryl's wounds were healing nicely. He had begun a therapy regimen and was beginning to use his right arm again. His leg had healed, but was stiff. The therapy was helping take the stiffness out of it. Mrs. Stevens was still there hovering over him like a mother hen, although he kept urging her to go back home. He told her he was getting better now and he would soon be well enough to take care of himself.

Darryl's sister, Carolyn, called one day to say that Darryl's father had fallen and needed her to come home and see about him. She was torn between staying with Darryl and going home, but Darryl finally talked her into going home to see about Mr. Stevens. Tammy volunteered to take Mrs. Stevens to the airport and Darryl gave a deep sigh, as he saw the car pull out of the driveway and head toward the airport. "I love you, Mom," he thought "but you were getting on my nerves."

When Mark got back home, he stopped by to check on Darryl. "When you have time, Mark, would you take me to the practice shooting range?" Darryl asked. "I need to get to where I can shoot again. I have to get back to work. I'm about to go stir crazy."

"Sure, I'll take you," Mark answered. "I have to go into the office and get my reports ready and see what's going on there first. I'll probably be able to take you in a few days. How will that be?"

"That's fine," Darryl answered.

So in a few days, Mark picked Darryl up and they headed to the shooting range. It was hard at first, but eventually Darryl was able to use his right arm and hit the target most of the time. Mark remembered the difficulty he had trying to use his left arm to shoot with. He could still recall the pain and frustration he had, trying to learn to use his left hand instead of his right one until his right arm healed.

The next week, Darryl went back to see his surgeon, who took X-rays and said that he was healing nicely. Next, he saw his physical therapist, who said that with a couple more weeks of therapy, he should be able to go back to work.

Mark told Darryl that when he was able to go back to work, he would need to get a form from his surgeon and one from his therapist stating that he was able to return to work. Then, he would have to take them to the Human Resources office before he could start back to work.

"Thanks for telling me," Darryl said. "I didn't know that."

"I didn't either until I tried to go back to work after my injuries healed," Mark said. "I found out in a hurry, though. I just didn't want you to find out the hard way, like I did."

The next week, Mark and his unit went out of state on an assignment and again the Styrofoam cup was left sitting on the bookcase shelf, forgotten.

After Mrs. Stevens was gone, Tammy made it a point to check on Darryl every day. Darryl began to have feelings for Tammy, the kind of feelings that made him want to be with her more and more.

One day, as she was helping him with his exercises, he pulled her to him and gave her a passionate kiss. She pulled away at first, then when he pulled her to him again, she didn't resist.

"I think I'm falling for you, Tammy," Darryl said, his voice husky with emotion.

"I think I'm falling for you, too, Darryl," Tammy answered breathlessly.

As he pulled her to him to kiss her again, she put her hands on his chest and stopped him. "Stop, Darryl," she said. "This isn't right. I can't fall in love with you. You're not what I want in a husband."

Darryl stopped and looked at Tammy with a startled look. "I didn't mean I wanted to marry you," he said. "I just want to make love to you."

Tammy gave him a disgusted look and said, "That's what I mean about your not being the kind of person I want for a husband. All you're interested in is sex. Forget it, I don't do sex outside of marriage. Since you've had sex with a lot of other women, I wouldn't even consider marrying you. I want my husband to be like me."

"Well, Lady," he answered angrily. "I don't think you're going to find someone like that. I didn't want to get married, anyway. I just wanted to make love to you."

"Well, you're out of luck, then," she said angrily and stalked out the door and slammed it behind her. "That man is impossible," she muttered to herself, as she wended her way through the hedge maze and back to Aunt Joy's house. She stomped through the door and slammed it.

"Tammy, is that you?" Aunt Joy called from the den.

"Yes, it is, Aunt Joy," she answered.

"What's wrong, Dear?" Aunt Joy asked. "Come here and tell me what's the matter."

"That neighbor of yours kissed me and tried to take me to bed," she answered, still mad, as she stomped into the den.

"You mean Darryl?" Aunt Joy asked.

"Yes, I mean Darryl," Tammy answered. "Who did you think I meant?"

"I warned you about him when you first came, remember?" Aunt Joy asked.

"Yes, I remember," Tammy said. "I just didn't expect it so soon. He sure doesn't waste time, does he?"

"He's getting better now, anyway. Maybe you should just stay away from him," Aunt Joy said.

"Don't worry. I will," Tammy said, as she sat down on the sofa next to Aunt Joy.

CHAPTER 15

THE DAY FINALLY came when Darryl was well enough to return to work. He did as Mark had told him and he got a form from his Primary Care Physician and one from his therapist stating that he was well enough to return to work. He then took the forms to the Human Resources office and was put back on the Active Employee list. It was almost September, so he would start working when the new month began.

While he was in the FSC Building, he decided to go by his office and tell them he would be starting to work in two weeks. Scott Harding, the Acting Commander, was sitting in Darryl's office when he arrived.

Scott stood and shook Darryl's hand as he entered the office. "Hello, Commander Stevens," Scott said. "Am I glad to see you."

"You sound like you're almost relieved that I'll be coming back," Darryl said. "You can call me Darryl, too, you don't have to call me Commander Stevens."

"I'll be glad when you return," Scott said. "Come on in and shut the door. I really need to talk to you."

"What's wrong?" Darryl asked, as he took a seat in front of Scott.

"I found out that I'm a follower and not a leader," Scott answered. "The team just about refused to do anything I said to do. I couldn't figure out the strategy for the assignments. If it hadn't been for Lee Garrison helping me, we wouldn't have accomplished anything.

"I decided I don't want to be SIC of this unit. I just want to be a member. I would like to suggest Lee, though, if you want a suggestion SIC. I think he would make a good one. I'll gladly hand you back the reins, when you return to work."

"Well, I'm glad to hear that I still have a job," Darryl said. "I'm sorry that you had such a bad experience, though. I'm glad in a way, though. Now I won't have to be afraid that you might want to take my job away from me."

"That'll never happen," Scott said. "Just hurry up and get back. The Director wants us to hurry up and start taking difficult assignments. I was afraid I'd have to do one before you got back."

"You make me feel good to know that you and the guys missed me," Darryl said. "Is there anything I can help you with while I'm here?"

"Yes, there sure is," Scott said, as he pulled out the procedure plan he had been working on. "I really need your help on this."

So Darryl and Scott worked on the procedure plan until noon. "Come on Scott, let's go to McDonald's and grab some lunch. I want to speak to everyone first and then we'll go, OK?" Darryl said, as he walked out the door.

At McDonald's, Mark Fuller and Jason Hall were sitting at a table together. When they saw Darryl and Scott enter, they called them and told them to join them at their table. When Darryl and Scott received their food, they sat down with Mark and Jason.

"Are you back at work already, Darryl?" Mark asked.

"Not yet," Darryl answered. "I just turned in my forms from my doctor and therapist. The lady in Human Resources said I could start in two weeks. I thought I would stop by the office and tell them the good news and see how things were going."

"That's great," Mark said. "I'm glad you're able to return so soon. I had to be off a lot longer than you did. I thought I would lose my mind before I was able to return."

"I would like for you to tell me about your accident some time when you have time," Darryl said to Mark.

"Just come by the house some time when I'm home," Mark answered. "I'll be happy to enlighten you."

Just then Darryl saw Cassidy sitting at the table with a man Darryl didn't know. "Who's the guy with Cassidy?" he asked Mark.

"That's Wayne Bennett," Mark answered. "He belongs to another unit. "I think they've been dating for a couple of weeks now."

"If you all will excuse me, I think I'll go over and say hi," Darryl said.

They all said sure go on over, so Darryl made his way over to Cassidy's table.

"Hello, Cassidy," he said, as he approached the table.

"Well, hello, Darryl," she answered, as her eyes lit up and she gave him a big smile. "Did you finally get well enough to come back to work?"

"Yeah, I start back in two weeks," he answered. "May I sit down for a few minutes?"

"Sure, go ahead," she said motioning to a seat. "Darryl, this is my friend, Wayne Bennett. Wayne, this is Darryl Stevens. Darryl is the Unit Commander of the unit that Scott Harding is Commanding right now. Darryl was wounded by sniper fire a few months ago and has been recuperating."

"Hello, Darryl," Wayne said, as he extended his hand to Darryl. "It's nice to meet you. Were you with the ones at the Academy? I heard about that. That was pretty bad."

"Yes, it was," Darryl said, as he lowered his eyes and took Wayne's hand. "Cassidy, the last time I saw you, we weren't on very good terms. I just wanted to say hi and say I still would like for us to be friends. There's no hard feelings, is there?"

"No, Darryl, there's no hard feelings," Cassidy answered. "As a matter of fact, I have to thank you. You made me see myself for who I was and I didn't like who I was, so I changed. I must say, I changed for the better. You like the new me, don't you, Wayne?"

"I sure do," Wayne answered enthusiastically.

"So, see, Darryl, there's no hard feelings and I still want to be your friend," Cassidy said.

Darryl smiled, said goodbye and walked back over to the table where Mark and the others were still sitting.

"Well, Darryl, unlike you, we working stiffs need to get back to work," Mark said, as Darryl sat down. "I would really like for you to come to dinner some time and really get to know my family. I think you'd like them and I know they'd like you."

"Sure, Mark, I'd like that. Just let me know when to come and I'll be there," Darryl answered.

"I'll talk to Cat and let you know, then," Mark said. "Now, I have to run."

"I do, too," Jason said, as he got up to leave.

"Jason, I'd like to talk to you some time when you have time," Darryl said. "Let me know when you have a few minutes."

"Sure," Jason said, as he walked toward the door. "I'll talk to you when you get back to work."

"Well, Scott, I guess that just leaves the two of us," Darryl said. "Is there anything else you need from me?"

"No, I think you did everything that I need for you to do," Scott answered. "I'll just be glad when you return in two weeks. I'll happily turn everything back over to you."

"I'll be glad to get back to work, too," Darryl replied. "While I'm here, I think I'll go see if I can see Director Halbert. I want to tell him I'll be back in two weeks."

When Darryl entered Director Halbert's office, he hoped that the Director would be available to see him. He asked the receptionist if he could see the Director.

"Just let me check," she said. She rang his phone and told the Director the Darryl wanted to see him.

"He said you can go in," the receptionist said, as she put the phone down.

"Thanks," Darryl said and he walked over to the Director's door. Director Halbert opened the door and said, "Come in, Darryl," as he held out his hand in a warm greeting. Darryl took his hand and continued on into the room.

"How are you doing, Darryl?" Director Halbert asked.

"I'm better," Darryl answered. "I've been released to go back to work in two weeks. I just thought I'd stop by and tell you personally."

"I'm glad you did," Director Halbert said. "Sit down."

They talked a while about how Darryl was doing, then Darryl asked, "How is the investigation going? Do they know who shot me yet?"

"No, Darryl, I'm sorry. They haven't been able to get any clues as to who shot you and killed the others," Director Halbert answered. "I know it must be frustrating for you. It's bad enough to be wounded like that, but to not have a clue as to who did it and why, it must be maddening."

"Yes, Sir, it is," Darryl answered. "Well, I guess I've taken up enough of your time. I guess I'll be going. I'll be back in two weeks."

He walked toward the door and Director Halbert followed him. "I'm glad you're able to return to work," he said. "I look forward to seeing what kind of Commander you make. I hope I'm not disappointed that I chose you over the other applicants."

Then he opened the door and Darryl left without making another comment. The Director's last comment hurt. It wasn't his fault that he had been injured and was unable to work. If it hadn't been for that, he would be doing his Commander job right now. In fact, if the Director hadn't insisted that he attend the Academy, he wouldn't have been wounded.

"I have to quit thinking like that," Darryl said to himself. "That could cause me to have hard feelings against the Director, and I shouldn't do that. I need to get along with him. I might need for him to do a favor for me sometime and it's best if we're on good terms with each other."

CHAPTER 16

DURING THE NEXT two weeks, Darryl was impatient to start work again. Now that his wounds had healed, he was anxious to prove to Director Halbert that he hadn't made a mistake in hiring him as Unit Commander. To pass the time away, Darryl did exercises to build up his strength and muscles. He also started running. He started at a mile a day and tried to build it up a mile every day. It was tiring, but it gave him a good feeling to know that he was improving every day.

He went over and visited Miss Joy and Tammy every now and then. He asked Tammy to go to dinner with him one day, but she turned him down. He wasn't what she was looking for in a husband, she had politely told him, and he wasn't interested in being a husband, so that was that. He still had a longing he couldn't describe when he looked at her, but he had to try to ignore it.

Mark Fuller had invited Darryl to come to dinner at his house one night. Cat had invited her sister, Carol and her family to come over as well.

As Darryl walked into Mark's house, he was greeted by Cat and the others. "I believe you've met Carol, Skip and their children, haven't you Darryl?" Mark asked.

"Yes, I believe I met them at church that day I was there," he answered. "Hello, everyone."

"Hello, Mr. Darryl, I'm glad you're feeling better," Sherry Rene said, as she shook his hand.

"Thank you, Sherry," Darryl answered.

"Why don't we sit down and visit for a while before we eat," Cat said. "I just put the rolls into the oven and they need to cook for about 25 minutes."

They all sat down and made small talk for a while. Sherry Rene had been sitting quietly observing everything, which was very unusual for her. Suddenly, she asked, "Mr. Darryl, why don't you go to church with us Sunday? I noticed that you haven't come the whole time you've been getting well."

"Well, I…" Darryl started slowly. "I really haven't felt like going to church," he finally managed to say.

"You're better now," she persisted. "Why don't you come Sunday? You liked it the time you came with Miss Joy, didn't you?"

"Yes, I did." Darryl didn't know what else to say. He had been caught off guard. He hated to say, "I don't do church." He didn't want to hurt Sherry's feelings, but he felt very uncomfortable talking about church. When he was a boy, his mother took him to church every Sunday. She always took him in time for Sunday School. When he became an adult, he drifted away from church, and now he didn't feel the need for it. He felt that church was only for children and parents of children. He was neither.

"Don't you think you need to go to church, Mr. Darryl?" Sherry began again.

Before he could answer, Skip said, "Sherry, leave Mr. Darryl alone. He'll go to church when he gets ready. You've invited him, now, that's enough. If he wants to come, he'll come."

"But he needs to go to church," Sherry insisted, and put on a grumpy face. "Mr. Darryl, will you come with me this Sunday?" she asked again. "My father's a preacher. He preaches at our church some times when Rev. Baxter is gone for some reason. Maybe you'll come sometime when he's preaching."

"I may do that, Sherry," Darryl answered, beginning to become calm again.

After dinner, they sat in the den and visited again. While the women cleaned up the kitchen, Mark gave Darryl an abbreviated version of his accident. "Wow, I can imagine how bad that must have been," Darryl said.

Darryl finally said that he was getting tired and needed to get on back home. "Thanks for inviting me," he said. "I really enjoyed it. I'll have to have all of you come to my place when I get back to normal."

"Be sure and try to come to church Sunday," Sherry called after him, as he was getting into his car.

"I will," he called back to her. As he started the engine, backed out of the driveway and headed home, he thought, "I will not. I don't think I'm ready to go to church yet. I think I'll have to wait on that."

When Sunday came, he stayed in bed intentionally longer than he usually did so he would have an excuse to miss church. He would say he overslept, if anyone asked him why he didn't come to church.

The telephone rang and he hesitated to answer it. It insistently kept ringing, so he dragged himself out of bed and answered it. It was Miss Joy.

"Good morning, Darryl," Miss Joy said, when he answered. "How are you this morning?"

"I'm fine," Darryl said hesitantly. He didn't know what Miss Joy wanted, but he was afraid he wasn't going to like it.

"Today is Tammy's birthday and I fixed her a special birthday dinner," Miss Joy continued. "I thought you might like to go to church with us this morning and then have lunch with us to celebrate Tammy's birthday."

"I just got up, Miss Joy," Darryl answered. "I'm afraid I would miss church by the time I get ready. I still have to shower and shave and then get dressed."

"We can skip Sunday School this morning and just go to church service. It doesn't start until 11:00. You'll have plenty of time to get dressed. I'll pick you up about 10:30, will you be ready by then?"

Darryl couldn't think of a polite way to decline, so he just said OK. Then he headed to the shower after hanging up the phone. "That woman will be the death of me yet," he mumbled to himself, as he undressed and turned on the water in the shower. When the water was warm enough, he climbed into the shower and let the warm water relax his tense body.

"Well, one good thing about this," Darryl thought, as he dried himself off. "I'll get to see Tammy again. Maybe she'll be more receptive to my invitation to take her out this time. Maybe she's mellowed with age," he chuckled to himself.

At 10:30 exactly, Miss Joy pulled into Darryl's driveway and honked her horn. Tammy sat in the back, leaving the front passenger seat for Darryl.

"Good morning, ladies," Darryl said, as he climbed into the car.

"Good morning, Darryl," they said in unison.

Tammy was wearing a powder blue dress, which set off her beautiful blue eyes. It had a V neck that plunged down to her breasts. Darryl let out a whistle, as he sat down. "If I'd known you dressed like that for church, I'd have gone with you more often," he said.

"Now, Darryl, mind your tongue," Miss Joy scolded him. "Remember, you're going to church."

"Sorry, Miss Joy, Tammy looks so good, though, I had to say something," he answered. "Happy birthday, Tammy."

"Thanks, I think," Tammy replied.

Miss Joy asked how Darryl was doing and the rest of the trip was centered around his recovery.

"When do you go back to work?" Miss Joy asked.

"Monday morning," Darryl answered. "I sure am looking forward to it, too. I couldn't stand being idle for another day."

As they arrived at the church, several couples were entering the building. Miss Joy introduced Darryl to them and they all walked into the church together.

"Maybe we can get together sometime," one of the men commented. "That would be nice," Darryl answered. That was all they could say because the service was starting as they all took their seats.

Sherry Rene turned around and saw Darryl and gave him an excited wave and he waved back. He could see her whisper something to Skip. Darryl figured that she had told him that he was there. He wanted to make it a point, later, to tell her he was there partly because she had invited him. That probably wasn't really a lie, anyway.

Rev. Baxter preached a stirring sermon on repentance of sin and salvation through the blood of Jesus Christ. Darryl uncomfortably stirred in his seat. He knew he was a sinner and needed to repent of his sins, but he just wasn't ready to make that commitment yet. He was glad when church was over and he didn't have to think about his sins any longer.

Sherry Rene ran up to him and hugged him. "I'm so glad you came, Mr. Darryl, did you enjoy it?"

Darryl knew he would hurt her feelings if he told her the truth and said, "No, I didn't enjoy it at all." So he just lied and said, "Yes, I really enjoyed it. Thanks for inviting me."

"Mr. Darryl, are you going to go to the restaurant and eat with us?" she asked.

"No, Sherry, not today," he answered. "Miss Joy invited me to eat with her and Tammy. Today's Tammy's birthday."

"I didn't know that," Sherry said. "I'll have to go wish her a happy birthday." Then off she skipped to find Tammy. She was back shortly, excitedly saying that Miss Joy had invited them to the birthday dinner, also. So now she would be able to eat dinner with Darryl after all. Darryl groaned, but didn't say anything. He hoped that the subject of church attendance didn't come up during dinner.

Miss Joy had cooked a large beef roast with plenty of carrots and potatoes cooked around it. She also had purplehull peas, fried okra, mashed potatoes and homemade yeast rolls. She had made gravy with the juice from the roast to top everything else off. She had cooked enough for an army it seemed like, so there was plenty enough to go around.

For dessert, Miss Joy had baked a large yellow sheet cake with chocolate icing and put one candle on top for Tammy to blow out and make a wish.

After everyone was stuffed, Miss Joy brought out the cake and lit the candle. "Now, Tammy," she said. "Close your eyes, make a wish and blow out your candle."

Tammy closed her eyes and thought for a while before blowing out the candle. Then she gave the candle flame a hard blow and out it went.

"Oh, Tammy," Sherry excitedly said. "You're gonna get your wish, you blew out the candle with one blow."

"I hope I get my wish," Tammy said, crossing her fingers.

"What was it?" Sherry asked.

"I'm not supposed to say," Tammy answered. "If I tell it, it won't come true."

"Aw, I wanted to know what you wished," Sherry said, as she pouted. Tammy didn't tell her, though.

After everyone finished their dessert, the men went into the den to watch a ball game and the women cleaned up the kitchen. Just as Darryl feared, the conversation turned to church.

"Darryl, have you ever accepted Jesus as your Savior?" Skip asked.

"I went to Sunday School and church both when I was a boy," Darryl answered. "My mom took me every Sunday, unless I was sick."

"That isn't what I asked you," Skip said. "I asked if you had repented of your sins and accepted Jesus as your Savior?" Skip asked again.

"I never have made a commitment," Darryl said, and he could feel the sweat running down his chest and popping out on his brow.

"Do you realize what your destination would be for eternity if you died today?" Skip continued to press Darryl.

"Look, Skip, I know it's your job to get everyone saved that you can, but I don't need to be saved. I'm OK with who I am. I don't need you to preach to me. Now, if you'll excuse me, I have to go home." Then he arose and headed to the door.

"Wait, Darryl," Skip called after him. "Just listen to me for a few minutes. I won't ask you to make a decision right now. I just want you to listen and think about how dangerous it is to put it off."

Skip was hoping that if he could get Darryl to listen long enough, the Holy Spirit would do His work of conviction and Darryl would see his need for a Savior.

But Darryl just kept walking and didn't stop until he was safely inside his door. He leaned against the door and wiped the sweat from his forehead with a trembling hand. "That's why I don't want to go to church," Darryl said to himself. "They always get around to your sins and your need to be saved. I'm OK like I am. I like my life like it is. I don't want to change. Maybe some day I will, but not now."

He removed his jacket and tie and threw them across a chair in his den. He sat down in his recliner and turned on the TV with the remote. He turned on the ball game that they had been watching, but he couldn't get interested in it. He turned it to another channel, but he still couldn't get interested in watching anything else.

Darryl finally turned the TV off and stood up and paced the room like a caged animal. "Why did I go over there?" he asked himself. "I should have known Miss Joy had an ulterior motive for inviting me. She intended for Skip to corner me like that. I should have known. I think they're all after me."

He finally wore himself out and sank back into his recliner exhausted. "I just won't go back to that church anymore," he thought. "I'll show them I'm OK. I don't need church, anyway."

The rest of his day was ruined. He couldn't think of anything except what Skip and Rev. Baxter had said. He argued with himself and said that he was OK and that he was satisfied with his life, but deep down, he knew he was only lying to himself.

CHAPTER 17

ON MONDAY MORNING, Darryl arose early, took a shower, shaved and dressed for work. As he was pulling out of his driveway, Tammy walked out of the house and waved to him.

"Hi, Tammy, how's everything going?" he asked. "Did you have a good birthday?"

"Yes, I did," she answered. "I'm just going shopping with some of my birthday money and gift cards. Are you going to work today?"

"Yes, I am," Darryl answered. "This is my first day back since my injury. I'm a little nervous."

"I hope everything goes well for you," she said, walking over to the side of his car.

"Would you like to go to dinner with me tonight to celebrate my return to work?" he asked, not really expecting her to agree.

"Sure, I'd like that," she answered. "What time?"

He was shocked that she would say yes, so he stammered a little and said, "What about 7:00? That'll give me time to get home and get ready. Is that OK with you?"

"Sure, 7:00 is fine with me," she answered.

"Well, bye until tonight, then," he said, as he started his car and drove out of the driveway.

Tammy watched as he drove off and said a prayer for him. She hoped that what Skip had said to him would sink in and he would see his need for Jesus. She smiled and thought, "I guess my wish is starting to come true after all. If I could just get Darryl to realize that he needs to be saved, it would really come true."

As Darryl was walking from the parking lot to the FSC Building, he heard a shot and felt a bullet whiz by his ear. He immediately dropped and rolled behind a bush and pulled out his revolver. "It must be the sniper from the Academy," Darryl thought. "I guess he came back to finish the job he started there."

He waited for a few minutes to see if the gunman would shoot again, then he cautiously inched his way toward the building. There were no more shots, so he hurried on into his office. He was shaking, as he opened his office door.

Scott Harding was waiting for him inside the office. "Good morning, Commander Stevens," Scott said. "It's good to have you back." When he saw how pale Darryl was and how his hands were shaking, he asked, "What's wrong?"

"Someone shot at me as I was walking into the building," Darryl answered.

"Did you see who it was?" Scott asked.

"No, whoever it was, was hidden and left after he shot one time. I don't know if that was supposed to just be a warning shot or if he was a bad shot and just missed. If it was meant to scare me, he succeeded."

As soon as Darryl calmed down, he called Director Halbert and reported it to him. "I'll notify the authorities," the Director said.

Soon, Detective Dan Urssery knocked on Darryl's office door. "Commander Stevens, may I come in?"

Darryl said yes and indicated a chair for the detective.

"I'm Detective Dan Urssery," he said. "I've been sent to question you about a shooting incident this morning. Will you tell me what happened?"

Darryl walked over to the door and closed it before he answered Detective Urssery. "I was walking from the parking lot to the building, when I heard a shot and something, I assume was a bullet, whizzed past my ear."

"Did you see who was doing the shooting," Detective Urssery asked.

"No Sir, I didn't," Darryl answered. "When I looked up, he was gone. I had ducked behind a bush and had drawn my weapon, but I didn't see anyone."

"Do you have any idea who might have wanted to shoot you? In other words, do you have any enemies?" Detective Urssery asked.

"Doesn't everyone have enemies?" Darryl asked. "In this business, anyway. I've only been here about four months and three of that was while I was recuperating from being shot before."

"Oh, yeah, that was the Academy shooting, wasn't it?" Detective Urssery asked. "Did they ever find out who did that?"

"Not to my knowledge," Darryl answered.

"Do you think the same person could have shot at you today? Maybe he came back to finish the job?" Detective Urssery asked.

"I thought about that," Darryl answered. "I don't know who it could be, though."

"Did you have enemies where you were before you came here?" the Detective asked.

"Well, yes," Darryl answered. "I arrested people in Florida. Some of them said they would get even with me. I'm sure you've had the same experience."

"Yes, I have," Detective Urssery said. "I need you to make a list of all of the people you can think of, who would want to see you dead."

"If you want everyone I've arrested, that'll be a long list. I can't remember everyone, either. Some of them are still in prison. It'll take me a long time to do that."

"Just give me a list of whoever you can remember and I'll get started checking them out," Detective Urssery said. "Did you ever think that maybe one of them could have been the shooter at the Academy?"

"No, it never dawned on me until today that this shooter could be the same one that was at the Academy. Why would he shoot the others, though, if he was aiming for me?" Darryl asked reflectively.

"Maybe he wasn't sure which one was you, so he shot all of you to make sure he got the right one. Or maybe he did that to throw you off and think it was just a random shooting," Detective Urssery said. "I'll check the security tapes and see if any of them caught your shooter. I'll also bring some photos by and see if you know any of the men in the mug shots of known felons in this area. If you think of anything, let me know. Here's my number. I'll be checking back with you about that list."

After Detective Urssery left, Darryl couldn't concentrate on his job. He kept running the shooting over and over in his mind. "Who would want to kill me?" he asked himself. There were plenty of men who probably hated him for having them arrested, but would one of them hate him enough to want to kill him? He started the list that Detective Urssery wanted and was surprised to realize that there were so many names on the list.

There was one name in particular that he underlined after he wrote it down---Derrick Lessing. Derrick was a small-time drug dealer who had begun to branch out into illegal weapons dealing. His weapons business had just taken off when Darryl had arrested him. Darryl remembered that on the day he arrested him, he had threatened to get even with him. He was given 20 years in the Federal prison in Florida. Surly he was still in prison. It hadn't been 20 years yet. He'd have to check on that.

Since this was Darryl's first day back at work after his injuries, Director Halbert called him into his office and told him that he wanted to start him off slowly, so he assigned a job of surveillance to Darryl and his unit.

There was a group of suspected terrorists that Director Halbert wanted Darryl's unit to keep an eye on. The Director thought that that would be the easiest job he could assign to Darryl's unit until Darryl was completely well enough to tackle the harder assignments.

After Darryl left the Director's office, he called his crew members together for a meeting to inform them of the Director's decision. "Everyone, in case you've forgotten, my name is Darryl Stevens. I'm your new Unit Commander," he started and everyone laughed.

"Director Halbert has given me a simple assignment to accomplish to help me get back into the swing of things. It's a simple surveillance job. I'm sure you have each done your share of surveillance jobs. Here's the site and the tentative schedule. We'll start Friday night. Look over the plan and, if you have any questions, feel free to come ask me, I'll be in my office. Yes, Dean, you have a question now?"

"Yes, Sir," Dean answered. "Your plan is different from what we've been doing. Do we need to change and do it the way you say do it?"

"Yes, Dean, you'll do it the way I say do it. In my experience, I have found this method to be the most useful. Do you have a problem with changing?"

"No, Sir," Dean answered. "I just wanted to be clear on it, that's all."

"Are there any more questions?" Darryl asked. When no one else asked a question, Darryl said, "You may go now. I'll be in my office if you need me." Then he turned and walked into his office.

A few minutes later, Scott Harding knocked on Darryl's office door. "Darryl, may I come in?" he asked.

"Sure, Scott, come on in and sit down," Darryl said, as he indicated a chair in front of his desk.

Scott shut the door and walked slowly over to the chair and sat down. He didn't say anything at first and Darryl said, "What do you have on your mind, Scott?"

"I don't really know how to say this, Darryl," Scott finally began. "I don't feel that I'm SIC material. I think you need to consider someone else, maybe Lee Garrison."

"Why do you feel that you're not SIC material, Scott?" Darryl asked.

Scott hesitated again before answering, then he slowly said, "The crew members don't respect me. They won't listen to what I say. They either ignore me or do exactly what I said not to do."

"Why do you think that is?" Darryl asked.

"Because I have always been a cut-up. I've been just one of the boys. I think they feel that I'm still just one of the boys. Maybe they're jealous. Maybe they feel that they could do a better job. Maybe they're right."

"Look, Scott," Darryl said. "I put you in charge because I felt that you were able to do the job. I care a great deal about my unit. I want my unit to be the best unit in the whole state, even the whole country. That's why I want the best SIC I can find to fill in for me when I'm unable to perform my duties. I feel that you're the best one for the position. Someone recommended Lee to me, but I felt that you were the best one. Will you be my SIC or do I need to ask Lee to be?"

"Since you put it that way, I guess I'll be your SIC," Scott answered.

"Then together we'll make this unit the best in the country, even if we do have to compete against Mark Fuller to do it," Darryl said. "If that's all, then go on back to work. I need to finish getting this surveillance schedule worked out."

Scott went back to his desk, satisfied that Darryl really wanted him for his Second-in-Command. He decided right then that he would make the best SIC that Darryl ever had. He would even strive to be the best one in the whole state and maybe the whole country.

Darryl was so engrossed in his work, that when 5:00 p.m. arrived, he didn't realize it was time to quit work and go home. He noticed that the office was quiet and he arose and looked out to find it was empty. "I guess it must be time to go home," he thought. So he finished what he was doing, turned out the lights and left.

As he was walking to his car, he felt something whiz by his ear and hit the tree next to him. He looked, but could not see anyone. Then another thing buzzed his ear and hit the building. He ducked behind the tree that had been hit and tried to see from where the shot had come. He couldn't see anyone, but he knew whoever had shot at him wasn't intending to hit him. Now he knew that whoever it was must have only been trying to frighten him. If the shooter had intended to hit him, he would have been an easy target. He was right out in the open and it would have taken a very poor marksman to have missed him twice. He was shaking, as he looked cautiously out of his hiding place. If the shooter was only trying to frighten him, as he thought, he had definitely succeeded.

Darryl went back into the FSC Building to report the shooting to Director Halbert, but he had already gone for the day, so he reported it to the Head of the Building Security, Joe Goode. "We'll look into it, Commander Stevens," Joe assured Darryl.

"You should be able to dig a bullet out of the tree out there. It sounded like it went into that tree," Darryl said, as he pointed to the tree where the bullet had hit.

"We'll take care of it, Commander," Joe said again. "Don't worry. If we can find out who's doing it, we will."

When Darryl arrived home, he was still a little unnerved. That was the third time he had been shot at. He realized that in his position, he would have to face gunfire, but he expected to be able to shoot back at whoever was shooting at him. This was frightening, though. Whoever this was had been hiding and he had no chance to return their gunfire. He just wondered if maybe the next time, the shooter wouldn't miss.

When he pulled into the driveway, Miss Joy and Tammy were sitting in the swing on Miss Joy's front porch. They waved and called out a greeting, as he exited his car. Darryl had been so involved with the shooting, that he had forgotten about asking Tammy to go to dinner with him, but he remembered when he saw her, so he made his way through the hedge maze and walked up the steps to the porch.

"Hello, Miss Joy, Tammy," he said.

"Hi, Darryl," Miss Joy said. "How was your first day back at work?"

"Pretty rough," Darryl said, as he sat down on the top step facing the two women.

"I figured you must have had a rough day, because you're as white as a sheet. Was it that hard getting back to work?" Miss Joy asked.

"No, Ma'am, it wasn't really that hard," Darryl answered. "I just had a bad incident on the way home. I'll be OK in a little while, I just need to rest for a while before our date, Tammy, if that's OK with you. Maybe I'm not as well as I thought I was."

"What happened?" Tammy asked. "We can make it another time, if you don't feel like going out tonight. Are you sure you're OK?"

"Yes, Tammy, I'm OK," Darryl answered, a little pleased that she sounded so concerned, but he avoided her question about what happened, anyway. He really didn't want her and Miss Joy to know that someone was still shooting at him. "I'll be OK after I rest for about 30 minutes. I still want to take you to dinner."

"Well, I hope you're well enough to get back to work," Tammy said. "You shouldn't go back before you're ready."

"Thanks for your concern," Darryl answered. "I think I'll make it OK now, though."

Then Darryl rose and started down the steps. "I'll go now, but I'll see you about 7:00, Tammy.

"OK, Darryl, I'll be ready and waiting," she answered with a smile.

Then Darryl went on down the steps and through the hedge in a lighter mood than he was in when he arrived home.

After Darryl rested for about 30 minutes, he had calmed down considerably. He took a hot shower and dressed in his nicest casual slacks and a short-sleeved shirt. He jumped into his car with a positive attitude and drove over to Miss Joy's house to pick up Tammy, who was waiting in the swing on the porch.

She was wearing a beautiful, frilly, red dress with a V neck. It wasn't a sexy cut that revealed too much of anything, though. It was cut just enough to show her nice figure. Darryl gave a wolf whistle when he saw her, causing her to blush.

"You look real nice, Tammy," he said as he walked up the stairs to take her by the arm and escort her to his waiting car.

"You look real nice yourself," she answered, as she walked by his side to the car.

As he drove to the restaurant, Darryl and Tammy had a pleasant conversation. At the restaurant, they continued their conversation and Tammy was beginning to be very comfortable with Darryl. She was beginning to hope that maybe he was changing and her birthday wish was coming true.

The next morning when Darryl arrived at the FSC Building, he looked around him cautiously before exiting his car, then he hurried inside the building. He didn't want a repeat of the incident of the night before. He knew that his luck would eventually run out and, if someone was really trying to kill him, they would eventually succeed.

That morning, he called his team together and presented his final surveillance plan to them. There were still some who didn't like his plan, but he was the Commander and what he said do, they would have to do.

Dean still questioned his method of doing the surveillance. "This is the way we've always done it," Dean said, as he showed Darryl a sketch of the way Jim Ryan and Mark Fuller had done the surveillance. "It has always been successful. I think we should continue to do it that way. That's the way we're familiar with."

"I'm the Commander, Dean," Darryl said with anger in his voice. "I have always done it this way and I'm familiar with it this way. I have always had success doing it this way and that's the way we'll do it. Do you understand?"

Dean just shook his head and walked off. He mumbled something under his breath that Darryl couldn't hear. Darryl was angry, but he hoped that Dean would soon give in and go along with him. He needed 100% participation or his plan wouldn't work

CHAPTER 18

WHEN MARK HEARD about Darryl's narrow escape again, he immediately thought about the Styrofoam cup that was still sitting on the shelf in his den. "I really need to get that cup to the lab and find out who that suspicious character was. Maybe he had something to do with the shooting at the Academy and shooting at Darryl recently. I'll take it to work with me tomorrow," Mark thought.

The next morning as Mark was ready to head out the door to go to work, he picked up the Styrofoam cup to take with him.

"Daddy, Daddy, give me kiss bye bye," little Jimmy Ryan called, as he ran to Mark with his arms outstretched. Mark turned to grab his son and just as he did, Jimmy tripped and fell, hitting his head against the coffee table. Blood immediately started oozing from the wound and Jimmy started wailing.

"My poor little boy," Mark said, as he grabbed Jimmy off of the floor and tried to console him. "Let Daddy see," Mark said, as he set the cup back in its former resting place on the shelf.

"Cat, Jimmy fell and cut his head," Mark called. "We need to get him to the hospital."

Cat came running with baby Crystal in her arms. She was so nervous, she couldn't think straight. "We need to drop Crystal off at Carol's on the way to the hospital. Maybe she won't mind taking care of her until we can get back," Cat said.

123

Mark grabbed some ice cubes out of the freezer, put them into a dishcloth and held them to Jimmy's head to try to stop the bleeding. All the time Jimmy was crying at the top of his lungs and tried to slap Mark's hand away. "Don't, Daddy, it hurts," Jimmy cried.

They finally got Jimmy into the car and stopped at Carol's to leave Crystal and headed to the hospital. At the hospital, Jimmy was immediately taken to an examination room with Cat following close behind. Mark stayed behind to fill out and sign the papers that were needed by the hospital.

After a couple of hours, Mark and Cat returned home with a small boy, who had a large bandage on his head and who was sleeping from the pain medicine given to him when the doctor had to put stitches in his wound.

Cat put Jimmy to bed while Mark went down to Carol's cabin and retrieved Crystal.

"What happened?" Carol wanted to know.

Mark told Carol about Jimmy's accident and thanked her for taking care of Crystal while they took Jimmy to the hospital.

"That's OK, Mark," Carol replied. "I was happy to do it. Sherry wasn't feeling well and I had already called the school and told them I wouldn't be in today. Let me know how he's doing tomorrow. Is there anything else I can do to help?"

"No, that's all that we needed, thanks," Mark answered. "I guess I'll go now. I need to get on in to the office and try to get half a day in, anyway."

From Carol's cabin, Mark went on back to take Crystal home and see if Cat needed for him to stay home.

"No, that's OK," she answered. "I can take care of things here. You just go on. I know you're busy."

Mark hurried out the door, jumped into his car and headed to his office; the Styrofoam cup was forgotten again.

Darryl's first couple of nights on surveillance were rough. When he sat for hours without moving, his shoulder and leg would get stiff. He tried moving around as much as he could, but he knew he needed to make as little movement as possible because he didn't want the suspects to notice him.

After the first two nights, he became adjusted to sitting hours at a time and was able to move just enough to keep from getting stiff. Darryl and Scott took one of the night shifts and slept during the day. They had some good conversations while they waited for their shift to end. They learned a lot about each other's lives, and soon became good friends. Scott learned that Darryl had only one sister and she was four years older than he was. Darryl also told him about his sister's two children, his niece and nephew, whom he doted on.

Scott, in return, told Darryl that he was the youngest of five children. He was the only single one in the family. His two brothers and two sisters all had children. Since he had no children of his own, he too doted on his nieces and nephews. They talked about other things that they had in common and decided to start doing things together when they had some time off.

Finally, Darryl felt that they had gathered enough information on the suspects to arrest them. He told his crew that the next morning they would raid the building they had been watching. Everyone was happy with that decision; they were glad that that assignment was finally coming to a close.

The next morning, all of the members of Darryl's unit met at the office and prepared to raid the suspects' building. They all put on their assault gear and loaded their weapons into their transport van.

When they arrived at the building, Darryl checked it out to make sure there wasn't a trap before his crew stormed into the building. Darryl decided to take it slow and easy to make sure there wasn't a bomb that would explode when they stormed the building. He remembered what Mark had told him about his accident.

When Darryl was sure that it was safe for them to do so, they stormed into the building with weapons drawn and shouted that they were Federal agents and for everyone to throw down their weapons and raise their hands above their heads. "Lay on the floor and put your hands behind your back," Darryl yelled to the suspects.

There was total confusion, as some of the suspects tried to get away and some refused to throw down their weapons and started firing at Darryl and his crew.

As Darryl was putting handcuffs on a suspect, another one of the suspects started creeping up on Darryl from the back. Just as he started to fire at Darryl, Scott saw the suspect and shot him. Startled, Darryl whirled around and saw the suspect on the floor with his weapon in his hand and Scott checking him for a pulse.

"Thanks for having my back, Scott," Darryl said. Then he turned and finished arresting the other suspects. Now Darryl felt that he had made the right decision when he had made Scott his SIC. He was glad that Scott had been there covering his back.

CHAPTER 19

THE NEXT WEEK was a busy week for Darryl's Unit. Director Halbert had seen that Darryl was able to handle an assignment now, so he was anxious to get his unit back into commission.

Most of Darryl's Unit had been with that unit when Jim Ryan was the Unit Commander, so they were familiar with North Korea. When another diplomat was kidnapped and taken prisoner by the North Koreans, the Director assigned the task of rescuing him to Darryl's Unit.

When Darryl got the assignment, he immediately called a meeting of his crew members.

"Some of you, I'm told, were with Jim Ryan when he rescued a diplomat from North Korea. Is this true?" Darryl asked.

Several of the men raised their hands and acknowledged the fact that they had been with Commander Ryan during that assignment.

"OK, I want each of you to write a report and include everything you can remember about that raid. I know that it's been over five years since that raid, but I want you to write as much as you can remember. When you're finished, we'll put all of the accounts together and maybe get a good picture of how it went down. I'll also talk to Mark Fuller, because I know he was with Commander Ryan when he led the raid. Now, are there any questions?"

"Yes, Commander Stevens," Scott asked. "When will we be required to go? I need to know how much time we have to prepare."

"We have two days," Darryl answered. "This is Monday, so we'll need to leave early Wednesday morning. Now, everyone get busy. This will be our test and I don't want us to fail. If we fail, we'll never get a second chance. You're dismissed."

Darryl went into his office and pulled the old files that contained the reports written by Jim Ryan and Mark Fuller after the accomplishment of that assignment. He was surprised to learn that Cat Ryan had been a participant in the raid. He read how there had been problems in rescuing the diplomat and Cat had been captured. Then, when Jim and Mark went back alone to rescue Cat, Jim was fatally wounded and died on the way back to the base.

"So that's how it happened," Darryl thought. "I never knew for sure how Jim Ryan died. I don't know if I should ask Mark to help me or not. It might dredge up old memories that are best left buried. I'll have to think about it and decide if I really need Mark's help or not."

On Tuesday, Darryl and Scott went to McDonald's for lunch. They were discussing the best strategy for rescuing the captured diplomat when Mark and Jason walked into the restaurant.

"Hi, Darryl, Scott," Mark and Jason said in unison. "May we join you two?"

"Hi, Mark, Jason. Sure, sit down," Darryl said.

"I heard you had an assignment in North Korea," Mark said. "I guess you know that Jason and I have been there."

"Yes. I read your report," Darryl said hesitantly. "I was debating about asking you for help. I didn't want to cause you any trouble, if it brought up some bad memories, though."

"That's OK, Darryl," Mark answered. "That was a long time ago. I still miss Jim, but Cat and I have to go on with our lives. I'll be happy to help you with your rescue plan, if you need me. I'll even go over with you, if Director Halbert OK's it."

"I would like for you to help me with the plan, since you've been there, but some of my crew were with you when you went, so I guess we can handle it. There's no need for you to go."

"I'll come by your office in about an hour," Mark said. "I just have to finish what I'm working on first."

After they were finished eating, Mark said, "I'll see you after while, Darryl." Then he and Jason walked out the door.

"I guess we need to go, too, Scott, since Mark will be over in an hour," Darryl said, as he stood and carried his trash to the trash receptacle.

Back at Darryl's office, he and Scott worked on a rescue plan. He wanted to at least be able to understand what Mark said about the North Korean compound when he arrived. Darryl had pulled up a map of the compound on his computer, so he had a good idea where the captured diplomat would be held.

When Mark arrived, he, Darryl and Scott were shut up in Darryl's office discussing the best plan to rescue the diplomat.

"You'll at least be better protected with the new gear you now have," Mark said. "If Jim and I had had this same gear, he would probably still be alive and I would still be single. But, that's all in the past, so now we need to think about the future. Here's how I think you should handle it."

Then Mark proceeded to explain how he would rescue the captive diplomat. By 4:00 p.m., Darryl had a plan, so he called his unit together and presented it to them.

"OK, you're dismissed," Darryl said after presenting his plan to them. "I want everyone here and ready to leave by 6:00 in the morning. If you're not here by then, we'll leave without you. You may leave now. I'll see you in the morning."

After all of his crew members were gone, Darryl shook Mark's hand and thanked him for his help. "I really appreciate your help, Mark. You don't know how relieved I feel, knowing that I have a definite plan that should work."

"I wish you luck, Darryl," Mark said. "Deep down, I have an urge to go with you, but I know Cat would throw a fit if I even suggested that I would like to go with you. I wouldn't even say anything to her about it. Well, I guess I'll head to the house. I'll see you when you return."

Early Wednesday morning, Darryl and his crew members loaded their transport van and headed to the base to begin their rescue assignment. It was a long trip to the drop site in North Korea, so Darryl had a lot of time to think. It wasn't that he was scared, but he was nervous. This would be his first real dangerous assignment after becoming Unit Commander.

Darryl wondered if he was up to the task. His shoulder still gave him some trouble and was still painful at times. When the weather was damp and cold, it was very painful. He knew that the weather in North Korea was probably going to be miserable, but he would just have to ignore the pain. After he became engaged in gunfire, he knew that the adrenaline would kick in and he would probably be feeling no pain.

Darryl didn't know why, but his thoughts turned to Rev. Baxter's sermon and then he thought about what Skip Taylor had said. Maybe when you were facing death, you started to wonder where you would spend eternity. He had been to Sunday School and church enough to know there was a Heaven and also a place called Hell.

Darryl never really thought about what his destination would be when he died; he never really even thought about dying, not until the sniper had begun shooting at him, that is. He decided right then that, if he got out of this alive, he would seriously think about asking Jesus to come into his heart. If God would just let him come out of this alive, he would seriously think about it.

Soon, they were landing in North Korea and all thoughts, except the ones concerning the rescue plan, were driven out of Darryl's mind.

The North Koreans were expecting them, of course, and there was a terrible gun battle. Several of Darryl's men were wounded and Darryl caught a bullet in his right leg, as he was hurrying the diplomat out of the compound.

They had to drop to the ground and spend about half an hour shooting it out with the North Koreans before they could get to the chopper and fly to safety.

"Thank you, Lord," Darryl said under his breath. He didn't even realize what he was saying, but he was relieved that God had protected him; he did know that much about God. He knew it was God who had brought him through it and he vowed to go to church Sunday, if he made it back alive, and do whatever he needed to do. He had a long trip back to the base to think about it.

Back at the base, Darryl and his wounded crew members received the medical attention they needed. The doctor told Darryl that he was lucky. He said that if the bullet had been just a little farther over, it would have hit his femoral artery and he would have probably bled to death before he could have gotten medical attention. That really made Darryl stop and think.

CHAPTER 20

DARRYL STAYED AT home for a few days to let his leg heal, but he was becoming bored, so he decided he would go to his office and write his report and send it to Director Halbert before he forgot some of the details.

Tammy had been coming over every day and checking on him, so he thought that he would go over to Miss Joy's house and tell them that he was going to return to work.

As he was starting out the door, a bullet whizzed by him and broke the window next to the door. Darryl ducked down and crept back into the house and grabbed his revolver.

When he exited the house again, there was another gunshot that broke another window. He searched the area all around his house, but he couldn't see anyone. He limped out to his car and saw that the back glass had also been broken. There was no sign of the shooter, though. Whoever it was, was still just trying to scare him.

Well, he was beginning to get really frightened now. The sniper was shooting at him in his own house; he was getting closer to him. "Who can this possibly be?" Darryl wondered. "Why is he just trying to scare me? Why can't I at least see who it is?"

When they heard the gunfire, Miss Joy and Tammy ran out of their house and asked Darryl what was going on.

"That sniper is shooting at me again," Darryl answered. "Miss

Joy, will you call the sheriff for me and report it? I would appreciate it if you will."

Miss Joy made the call and Tammy had Darryl sit down on the steps and she put her arm around his shoulders and tried to calm him down.

After the sheriff came and did his investigation, Darryl said he needed to go into the office for a while. When he was sitting in his office, he was still too shaken up to write his report about the North Korean assignment, so he decided to go to Mark's office to talk to him.

"Hello, Mark, may I talk to you for a few minutes?" Darryl asked, as he knocked on Mark's office door.

"Sure, Darryl, come on in and shut the door," Mark answered. "Sit down. What can I do for you?"

"I don't know how to begin," Darryl started, as he sat down in a chair in front of Mark's desk.

"Well, just tell me what you have on your mind and we'll go from there," Mark said, encouraging Darryl to continue.

"Mark, I was really scared on the flight over to North Korea," Darryl began again.

"That's only logical, Darryl," Mark said sympathetically. "This was your first really dangerous mission as a UC wasn't it?"

"Yes, it was, but that wasn't it," Darryl said, fidgeting in his seat.

"What was it then," Mark asked, as he leaned back in his chair.

"I had a lot of time to think and I started thinking about what Skip and Rev. Baxter said. About my soul; you know what I mean?"

"Yes, Darryl, I know exactly what you mean; I've been there, too," Mark answered, a thrill running through him, as he comprehended what Darryl meant.

"Well, I started thinking about what would happen to me after I die," Darryl continued. "I think I need to find out what I need to do to get right with God."

"I'm glad you're finally thinking about eternity, Darryl," Mark

133

said, as he stood, walked over to his bookcase and walked back to his desk with a copy of the King James Version of the *Holy Bible.*

"The first thing you have to do, is admit that you are a sinner. Let me show you this verse, Romans 3:23 **'For all have sinned, and come short of the glory of God.'** That means that everyone, you included, are sinners. When you realize this, then you need to know that there is a way to become clean. Romans 5:8 gives us the solution to our sin problem. It reads, **'But God commendeth his love toward us, in that, while we were yet sinners, Christ died for us.'**

"Now that you know there is a solution, Darryl, you need to know what you must do to apply that remedy to your own condition. Look at this verse, Darryl. Romans 10:13 says, **'For whosoever shall call upon the name of the Lord shall be saved.'**

"Darryl, this is my favorite verse right here. To me, it is the most beautiful verse in the Bible It is John 3:16, **'For God so loved the world, that he gave his only begotten Son, that whosoever believeth in him should not perish, but have everlasting life.'**

"All you have to do is believe that Jesus is the Son of God and that He can forgive you of all of your sins. Then repent of your sins and accept Him as your Savior. That's all you have to do."

When Mark was finished, Darryl had tears in his eyes. "I know that I am a sinner and that Jesus can forgive me of all my sins. What do I do now, Mark?" Darryl asked as he wiped his eyes of tears.

"Now, you need to pray and ask God to forgive you of your sins and trust Him as your Savior. Do you want me to kneel and pray with you?"

"Yes, Mark, I'd like that," Darryl said, as he and Mark knelt and prayed together.

When Darryl rose, he felt a peace that he had never felt before. "Thank you, Mark. I'm not afraid anymore. I now know what my destination will be, if I die tomorrow, which I might do, if that sniper continues to shoot at me. He'll probably get me the next time."

"That reminds me," Mark said. "I keep forgetting to bring

something to the lab to be tested. I'll do that in the morning. Maybe that suspicious character I saw had something to do with those shootings. I'll let you know what I find out."

When Mark got home that afternoon, he put the Styrofoam cup next to his car keys, so he wouldn't forget it the next morning when he went to work.

As soon as Mark arrived at his office the next day, he went directly to the lab. "I'd like to have this checked for DNA, if you can," he asked the lab technician. "I believe this person is responsible for the deaths of four FSC agents and the serious wounding of another one. Can you get this for me as soon as possible?"

"Sure, Commander Fuller," the technician answered, as he took the Styrofoam cup and made a label for it. "Let me have your office number and I'll let you know as soon as I find out something. If your suspect has been in jail, we should have something on him."

That same morning, Darryl decided to try to go to his office again. He cautiously inched his way out to his car and got into the driver's seat. He breathed a sign of relief when he made it safely there without being shot at. "I need to take my car to the glass repair shop and get a new window put in it," Darryl thought, as he drove out of the driveway and on toward his office.

Darryl decided to go by his office first and see if someone would go with him to the glass repair shop. That way, he would have a ride back to the office. Scott volunteered, but Darryl said he needed to be in the office in case something came up. When Lee Garrison heard the discussion, he volunteered to go.

Darryl left his car at the repair shop and got into Lee's car. On the way back to the office, Darryl asked Lee why he was against Scott becoming SIC.

"I really like Scott," Lee answered. "I don't really have anything against him as a person. He just isn't strong enough to be SIC. He isn't a good leader. I would hesitate to follow him because he always seems so unsure of himself. Would you follow someone who acted like he didn't know where to go and what to do after he got there?"

"He can't be that bad," Darryl commented. "He told me he had filled in for Jason Hall a few times. Surely he obtained some experience in leading then."

"He didn't do it by himself," Lee answered. "I was always there to help him. If you make him your SIC, I probably won't be able to be there to hold his hand every time he needs me."

"Why didn't you tell me this when I asked you before?" Darryl asked.

"I don't know. I just didn't want you to think I was trying to put Scott down so you'd give me the position," Lee answered.

"I've already made Scott my temporary SIC. He impressed me when he covered my back on the suspected terrorist surveillance job we just completed. I'll probably give him a few weeks trial period before I make it official, though. If during that time you feel that Scott isn't performing as he should, I want you to bring it to my attention. Then, we'll go from there. Right now, though, Scott is my SIC and I expect you and the others to respect him as such. Thanks for the information. Thanks, also for the lift, I'll need another one when my car's ready, if you're available then," Darryl said, as he exited Lee's car.

This conversation with Lee irritated Darryl. Now he had doubts as to the ability of Scott to carry out the duties of SIC. He felt sure that Scott was capable after he had covered him when they were arresting the suspected terrorists, but now he wondered if he would be capable to lead the unit if Darryl was ever unable to perform his duties. Well, he had told Lee that he would give Scott a trial run. At the end of that trial, Darryl would see whether Scott would be able to do the job or not.

Darryl had other things to think about now. He had to write a report on the North Korean assignment while it was still fresh in his mind. Since the surveillance job was over, now he could ask Tammy out again, so he was thinking about that, also. "When I get home, I'll see if Tammy wants to go to a movie this Friday night," he thought.

CHAPTER 21

BY FRIDAY, MARK still hadn't gotten a lab report on the Styrofoam cup, so he called to see if they were finished with it yet.

"We're almost finished with it, Commander Fuller," the lab technician answered. "We should have it completed by this afternoon. I'll get you the results as soon as the report is complete."

"Thanks," Mark answered. "Let me know as soon as you can, then."

Since Darryl was going to take Tammy to a movie, he decided to take off work early. That way he could get ready at his leisure and not have to be rushed. He wanted everything to be perfect for his date with Tammy. He had been thinking of her a lot lately, maybe more than he should. Sometimes he even thought that, if he ever did think about getting married, which he felt probably would never happen, then Tammy would probably be the one that he would want to marry.

Tammy saw Darryl drive into his driveway and wanted to ask him something about their date, so she happily made her way through the hedge maze, up Darryl's steps and knocked on his door.

Darryl answered the door, surprised to see Tammy there. "Tammy, I didn't expect to see you already. I'm not ready yet. I still have to shower and get ready," he said as he gave her a quick kiss.

"That's OK, Darryl," she answered. "I'm not ready to go yet, either. I just had a few questions I wanted to ask you."

"Come on into the den and sit down," Darryl said, as he led her into the den.

Suddenly there was a loud knock on Darryl's front door. "I wonder who that can be," he said. "Excuse me, Tammy, while I go see who it is and what they want."

When he opened the door, he was shocked to see a large, muscular man holding a shotgun. "Hello, Commander Stevens," the man sneered, as he pushed Darryl out of the way and walked into the house without being invited in.

"Do you remember me, Commander Stevens?" The man almost spat out Darryl's name. "It's Derrick Lessing, just in case you don't recognize me."

Then Derrick stuck the shotgun in Darryl's chest and urged him toward the den.

"My, what do we have here?" Derrick said when he saw Tammy, who had stood when she heard Derrick making his way toward the den. "What a pretty young lady. Is she your girlfriend, Commander Stevens? Or maybe your wife? You know I didn't get to see my wife for many years because of you. During that long time, she got tired of waiting and left me. Do you know how that makes you feel, to have your wife leave you? Well, it's awful. Is this your wife, Commander Stevens?"

"No, she isn't my wife," Darryl answered. He was afraid of what Lessing had planned for him and he sure didn't want Tammy to be a part of it. "She's just my next door neighbor's niece. She just came over to bring me something. Leave her alone. She has nothing to do with your being in prison."

"Oh, you want me to leave her alone, huh?" Derrick said with a sneer. "Well, maybe I don't want to leave her alone. Maybe I'll just have a little fun with her before I get rid of you."

"Leave her alone, Lessing," Darryl said, as he took a step toward Derrick.

Derrick hit Darryl on the head with the butt of the shotgun and Darryl fell to the floor and Tammy screamed.

"Shut up, girl, or I'll give you some, too," Derrick said, as he pointed the weapon at Tammy. "Now, you just sit back down and be quiet."

"Darryl's head is bleeding," Tammy said, as she started toward Darryl. "Let me try to stop the bleeding."

"That's OK, girl. Pretty soon he's gonna be bleeding even more. So you just sit down and be quiet like I said. OK, Commander Stevens, get up," Derrick said, as he kicked Darryl in the ribs. "You get over there and sit next to your girlfriend or wife. What is she, anyway, and what's her name? I don't want to keep calling her girl."

"My name's Tammy," she said before Darryl could say anything. "Like he said, I'm his neighbor's niece. I just came over to bring him the newspaper. I need to go on back before my aunt wonders where I am."

"No, you don't, Miss Tammy," Derrick said grinning at Tammy. "You think I'm stupid or something. You think I'll let you go and you'll call the cops. No way, you just keep sitting right where you are until I'm through with Commander Stevens.

"Now, Commander Stevens, I'm through playing with you," Derrick said, as he waved the gun under Darryl's nose. "I guess you've figured out by now that it was me shooting at you. Well, if you haven't, I'm the one. I thought I got you at the Academy. I didn't know for sure which one was you, but I knew you were one of the ones on the stage. I hated to have to shoot all of them, but I wanted to make sure I got you. Just my luck, you were the last one and I got all of them but you.

"Then, I decided it would be fun to play with you for a while before I killed you. You should have seen your face that first day I shot at you," Derrick said, as he laughed at Darryl. "You were white as a sheet and shaking like a leaf. Big, strong Unit Commander. You were almost scared to death. Now, you know how I felt while I was in prison. I feared for my life every day."

Darryl again tried to reason with Derrick. "Please let Tammy go. She had nothing to do with your going to prison. That was in Florida and it was a long time ago. Please let her go."

"Oh, I like that," Derrick said, as he stuck the gun into Darryl's chest again. "You even said please; that's really nice of you. You weren't that nice when you arrested me. You weren't nice at all, you remember, you shoved me," Derrick said, as he roughly gave Darryl a shove and he fell against Tammy.

"Sorry about that, Miss Tammy," Derrick said. "It's too bad you were here. I really didn't want to hurt anyone else, just this piece of trash. You understand why I can't let you go, don't you, Miss Tammy. You see, when I get through playing with Commander Stevens, here, I'm gonna kill him. Now, when you see me kill him, you'll be a witness. You understand, I can't have a witness, don't you?"

"Yes, I understand," Tammy said with a shaky voice. "I think it would be better if you didn't kill him, then you won't have to kill me. Then we'll all be better off."

Derrick started to laugh again. "You're really something, Miss Tammy," Derrick said. "You really think I'll forget about killing Commander Stevens after all this planning I've done? You can't be serious."

"Come on, Lessing," Darryl tried again. "You don't really want to kill Tammy, do you? Why don't you let her go, if she promises not to call the police. If she doesn't see you kill me, then she can't testify against you, see."

"But she is going to see me kill you," Derrick said. "Because I am going to kill you and she's gonna be here while I do it."

"Please let her go, Lessing," Darryl pleaded. "She'll promise not to call the police until after you get away, won't you, Tammy? Tell him you won't call the police until he has time to get away."

"Shut up, Stevens," Derrick shouted and hit Darryl with the gun again. "She can promise all she wants to, but she ain't goin' nowhere."

Then Darryl's phone began to ring. "Let it go to voice mail," Derrick said.

"Darryl, this is Mark Fuller. I got that lab report back. That character I told you about was a guy named Derrick Lessing. Didn't you have his name on your list? Call me and let me know. I need to know as soon as possible," Mark left a message for Darryl when he didn't answer the phone.

"What list is that, Commander Stevens?" Derrick asked.

"Just some names of people I've arrested," Darryl said, as he held his handkerchief to his head to stop the bleeding.

"Yeah, who else is on that list?" Derrick asked.

"I don't remember," Darryl answered.

"What character is he talking about?" Derrick wanted to know.

"Some guy he saw at the airport," Darryl answered.

"I was at the airport a while back. How did he get my name?" Derrick asked again.

"He saw you and thought you looked suspicious. So he ran your prints to see who you were," Darryl answered.

"How did he get my prints?" Derrick was getting agitated now.

"He got them off of a cup you threw away," Darryl said.

"How'd he do that?" Derrick wanted to know.

"I don't know. You'll have to ask him," Darryl said.

"Well, I just might have to do that, smart ass," Derrick said and then he slapped Darryl in the mouth. "Who is this Mark whatever-his-name-is, anyway?"

"He's a Unit Commander like I am," Darryl answered. He was beginning to get weak from loss of blood. Tammy held her hand to his head and tried to stop the blood, but she wasn't having much luck at stopping it.

"Stop that, Tammy," Derrick said, as he pulled her hand away from Darryl's head. "Leave it be. I told you he's gonna be bleeding more after while, anyway. When I get tired of playing with him, I'm gonna kill him."

When Mark couldn't get Darryl on his cell phone, he decided to call Detective Dan Urssery, who had investigated the first time the sniper shot at Darryl in the FSC Building parking lot.

"Detective Urssery, this is Unit Commander Mark Fuller. I believe you investigated a shooting at our FSC Building a short time ago, am I correct?"

"Yes, Commander Fuller, I did," Detective Urssery answered, wondering what Mark was getting at.

"Do you still have that list of suspects you had Commander Stevens write for you?" Mark asked.

"Yes, I do, it's here in my file. What do you need?" Detective Urssery asked.

"Would you look on it and see if there's a man named Derrick Lessing on it?" Mark asked.

"That name sounds familiar," Detective Urssery said, as he got the list out of the file. "Here it is, let me see. Yes, here it is. As a matter of fact, it's underlined. What about him?"

"I think he may be the one who's been shooting at Commander Stevens. I've been trying to get him on the phone, but my call just keeps going to voice mail. I think I'll run by his house and see if something's wrong. It's not too much out of my way home," Mark answered, then hurriedly got off the phone, so he could be on his way to Darryl's house.

Aunt Joy was beginning to get concerned about Tammy. She was only going to run over and ask Darryl about the movie they were going to see and then run back and get ready for their date. Now she had been gone for almost an hour. The movie would be starting before they could get there if they didn't hurry. She called Tammy's phone, but she got no answer. The call eventually went to voice mail.

"Tammy, what's keeping you?" Miss Joy asked, after the beep. "I hope you're not doing something you shouldn't be doing. Answer me."

She waited for a few minutes and then she called again. There was still no answer. This time when she left a message, she said,

"Tammy, if you don't call me back, I'm coming over there and find out why you're not answering your phone."

"Answer the damn phone," Derrick said when Aunt Joy called again. "Don't say anything that will make her suspicious, though."

"Hello, Aunt Joy," Tammy said, her voice shaky. "It's OK. We decided to stay here instead of going to the movie. I'll be home after while."

"I think you need to come on home right now," Aunt Joy said with a stern voice. "I don't like the idea of your staying over there like that."

"I'm OK, Aunt Joyce, just stay there. I'll be home shortly," Tammy hoped that Aunt Joy would notice she had called her Aunt Joyce and would understand that something was wrong.

"Now that's odd," Aunt Joy said to herself. "She's never called me Aunt Joyce before. Something must be wrong."

Then she called Mark to see if he would stop by on his way home from work. "Mark, I hate to bother you, but I think something's going on over at Darryl's house. Could you stop by on your way home and check for me?"

"What sort of thing do you think is going on, Miss Joy?" Mark asked.

"Well, Tammy went over there about an hour ago and said she was just going to be a few minutes. I called her phone and she didn't answer at first. When she did answer, she called me Aunt Joyce. She's never called me Aunt Joyce before."

"I think you're right, Miss Joy," Mark said. "I've tried to call Darryl several times and he doesn't answer his phone. I think I'll call his unit's SIC and see if I can get them over here, too."

By the time Mark had reached Darryl's house, he had alerted Scott Harding and Scott said that he would get the unit together and make their way to Darryl's house.

Mark drew his weapon and knocked on Darryl's door. "Darryl, it's me, Mark Fuller, can I come in?" Mark called, then stepped away from the door in case Lessing shot toward the door.

"Go away, Mark," Darryl called. "I can't let you in right now."

"Is Lessing in there with you?" Mark called through the door.

"Yes, he is," Darryl called. "He's holding me and Tammy hostage. Go away."

"I can't do that, Darryl. Lessing, we need to talk. Can you hear me?" Mark shouted.

"Yeah, I can hear you," Lessing shouted. "Go away or I shoot the girl."

"You don't want to do that, Lessing," Mark shouted. "Let the girl go, she hasn't done anything to you."

By now, Scott Harding and Darryl's unit had arrived with their assault gear. Mark walked over to Scott to tell him the situation.

"Derrick Lessing, an ex-con that Darryl arrested and put into prison, is holding Darryl and Miss Joy's niece, Tammy. He said if I don't go away, he'll shoot the girl. Do you have an idea how we can get him before he shoots one of them?"

"I don't know, Commander Fuller," Scott said. "I've never handled a hostage situation before. Do you think we can sneak up on him from the back?"

"I don't know," Mark answered. "I just got here, I haven't had time to assess the situation yet."

"I'll take a couple of my crew and go around the back and see what it looks like back there," Scott said, as he motioned to two of his crew to follow him. "You stay here and keep him occupied."

"Hey, Lessing," Mark called. "I need to talk to you. Will you come to the door, so I don't have to keep yelling?"

"That's funny, Commander, you think I'm gonna fall for that? You want me to come out there so you can shoot me. I'm not that stupid. Now if you don't leave, I'm gonna shoot the girl. I mean it, now leave."

"You don't really want to shoot the girl," Mark shouted. "She's never done anything to you. Why don't you just let her go?"

"Because I kinda like having her around," Lessing called back. "She's pretty. She's nice and soft," Lessing said, as he ran his finger over Tammy's cheek and felt of her shoulder. "I think I'll just keep her for a while. You know I've been in prison for a long time. I really think I'll keep her."

As Lessing put his arm around Tammy's shoulders and pulled her to him, Darryl jumped up and shouted, "Leave her alone, Lessing. Let her go. It's me you want, not her. Let her go."

Lessing hit Darryl with the gun again and knocked him to the floor. "I'm not through playing with you, yet, Commander Stevens. You'll get your turn. Just sit down and shut up. You're not in control here. I am."

Then Lessing heard a noise from the back. "You sit down and don't move," he said to Darryl and Tammy. "I'll go check that out. You better hope it's not some of your buddies trying to sneak up behind me. I'll get them before they can get in the back door."

Darryl and Tammy were startled by rapid gunfire and then Lessing rushed into the room and grabbed Tammy and held her to his chest. "Don't come any farther or the girl gets it," he said. "I mean it. Drop your weapons."

Darryl turned to face the back of the room and saw Scott Harding charging into the room. Lessing fired at Scott at the same time that Scott fired at Lessing. Lessing fell to the floor dragging Tammy with him.

Tammy screamed and Darryl ran to her and pulled her away from the wounded Lessing. "I'll still get you," Lessing said, as he aimed his weapon at Darryl. Before he could fire, Scott shot Lessing again. This time, Lessing lay motionless on the floor, blood was oozing from his wound.

Scott hurried over to Darryl, who was holding a sobbing Tammy to his chest, trying to comfort her.

"You OK, Commander Stevens?" Scott asked.

"I guess I'm as OK as I can be," he answered with a weak voice. "Are you OK, Tammy."

"I'm OK, now," she said through sniffles. "Is it all over?"

"I think so," Darryl said, hugging Tammy to his chest.

Then Mark and the other crew members broke through the front door. They saw Lessing on the floor and Mark hurried over and took his weapon from his hand and checked his pulse. "I think he's gone," Mark said, as he walked over to Darryl and Tammy. "You two OK?" he asked. "Looks like you need something done to your head, Darryl."

"I'm OK, now. Thanks for rescuing us," Darryl said "I really thought we were done for."

"Was he the only one?" Mark asked, as Scott and the rest of the unit began searching Darryl's house for other gunmen.

"Yeah, he was alone," Darryl said. "He was just trying to get even with me for sending him to prison."

"I think we need to notify the sheriff's office and let them know what's happened here," Mark said, as he took out his phone and punched in the number. "You two need to sit down. The medical personnel will be here shortly. Here hold this handkerchief on that wound to try and stop the bleeding until they get here."

Shortly, an ambulance arrived and the EMT's doctored Darryl's wounds and checked to see if Tammy was wounded. She had only some minor cuts and bruises and carpet burns where she had fallen when Lessing had dragged her down when he fell.

"You go on to the hospital in the ambulance, Darryl," Mark said. "I'll take care of things here. They can go to the hospital and get your statement. You need to go, too, Tammy. It won't hurt for you to get checked out, too."

"I need to call Aunt Joy first," Tammy said, as she pulled out her phone and made her call. When Tammy told Aunt Joy that she was going to the hospital just to get checked out, she said, "Wait a minute, I'll be over there in my car. You'll need a ride home."

Darryl and Tammy were taken away to the hospital and Mark, Scott and the rest of Darryl's unit stayed and finished up with the sheriff.

It was very late when Miss Joy finally arrived back at home with Darryl and Tammy. Mark had called Cat and given her a brief rundown of what had happened and told her he would be really late getting home.

Finally, at 3:00 a.m., they all fell into their own beds, exhausted. They didn't get much sleep, but at least they were all back at home in their own beds.

CHAPTER 22

DARRYL, TAMMY AND Miss Joy attended church on Sunday morning following the hostage situation. They wanted to let God know how thankful they were for His care and protection all through their terrible ordeal. While at church, Darryl and Tammy continued to thank Mark for his involvement in their rescue.

After services that morning, Darryl presented himself as a candidate for baptism and for membership into the Friendship Baptist Church. When the vote was taken, there was no opposition at all, so it was decided that his baptism would take place the following Sunday morning after services.

On Monday morning, even though Darryl was wounded and still weak and shaken up, he went to the office to officially thank his team for rescuing him and Tammy.

He waited in his office for his unit members to arrive. After they had all arrived, he called a meeting in the conference room.

"Everyone," Darryl began. "I want to express to you how grateful I am for your rescue. I also want to let you know how proud I am of each one of you. I especially want to thank Scott for taking charge of the rescue. You did an excellent job, Scott. I just want to tell you that I have no doubts as to your ability to handle the job of SIC from now on. The job is officially yours. I'll turn in the paperwork today."

The following Sunday, after services, Darryl was baptized and became a member of Friendship Baptist church. Tammy decided she would stay with Aunt Joy for a while, so she decided to move her letter from her home church to Friendship Church, too.

After Darryl's baptism, Tammy and Darryl were presented to the congregation, who came by and shook their hands and welcomed them into their church family.

On the way home from church, Tammy thought, "My birthday wish is finally coming true. Now that Darryl has surrendered himself to the Lord, he will be more like the man I would choose for my husband."

In the weeks and months following, Tammy and Darryl spent as much time together as they could. When Darryl wasn't on an assignment, he and Tammy were together. They were fast falling in love.

One beautiful Spring night, as Darryl and Tammy sat in the swing on Aunt Joy's porch, Darryl got down on one knee, took Tammy's hand in his and said, "Tammy, my love, will you do me the honor of becoming my wife?"

"Yes, of course," Tammy said with tears in her eyes. "I would love to be your wife."

Then Darryl took out a small velvet box, opened it and slipped a beautiful diamond ring on Tammy's finger. Then he stood, pulled Tammy into his arms and kissed her passionately.

"Tammy, you have made me the happiest man alive," he said.

"You've made me the happiest girl, too," Tammy answered. "I have to go tell Aunt Joy."

When Tammy and Darryl told Aunt Joy, she joined in their happiness. "I've always wanted to plan a wedding," Aunt Joy said. "I can hardly wait."

That night, Darryl called his parents and told them the good news. His mother could hardly wait to tell Darryl's sister and all the rest of the family. "When can I come and help get things ready?" she asked.

"You can call Tammy tomorrow and ask her," he answered. "I'll let you, Tammy and Miss Joy take care of that."

As Darryl lay in his bed that night, he thanked God for all that He had done for him. "Thank you God for Your Son, Jesus Christ, who died on the cross to pay my sin debt for me. Thank You for saving my soul and protecting me through all that I've been through. Most of all, thank You for Tammy, my beautiful, Christian, soon-to-be wife."

As he drifted off to sleep, Darryl thought about all that he had been through since he had arrived at his new home and his new job. Now he realized that God had been there the whole time, just waiting for Darryl to find Him and accept Him as his Savior. "He even had it planned for Tammy to be my wife," Darryl thought. "Thank You, God. Thank You for everything."

Then he fell asleep with a huge smile on his face and peace in his heart.

Printed in the United States
By Bookmasters

Headscarf